THE END OF THE AFFAIR

A NOVEL

BY GRAHAM GREENE

NOVELS

The Man Within
It's a Battlefield
The Shipwrecked
*Brighton Rock
*The Heart of the Matter
Orient Express
Loser Takes All
*Our Man in Havana
Triple Pursuit (*This Gun
for Hire, The Third Man,
Our Man in Havana*)

*The Power and the Glory
'The End of the Affair
*The Quiet American
*A Burnt-Out Case
*The Comedians
The Third Man
Travels with My Aunt
*Three by Graham Greene
(*This Gun for Hire,
The Confidential Agent,
The Ministry of Fear*)

TRAVEL

In Search of a Character
*Another Mexico

*Journey without Maps

SHORT STORIES

A Sense of Reality
May We Borrow Your Husband?

*Twenty-One Stories

ESSAYS AND AUTOBIOGRAPHY

*The Lost Childhood
Collected Essays

A Sort of Life

PLAYS

The Living Room
*The Potting Shed

The Complaisant Lover

VIKING CRITICAL EDITION

The Power and the Glory (*edited by
R. W. B. Lewis and Peter J. Conn*)

Available in Viking Compass edition.

Graham Greene

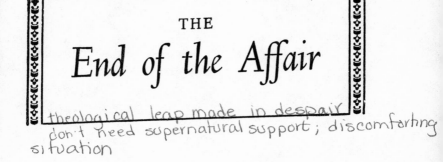

THE

End of the Affair

theological leap made in despair don't need supernatural support; discomforting situation

New York

THE VIKING PRESS

VIKING COMPASS EDITION

Issued in 1961 by The Viking Press, Inc.

625 Madison Avenue, New York, N.Y. 10022

Thirteenth printing April 1973

SBN 670-29457-8 (hardbound)

SBN 670-00083-3 (paperback)

Library of Congress catalog card number: 51-13559

Printed in the U.S.A. by The Colonial Press Inc.

TO CATHERINE
with love

THE END OF THE AFFAIR

Man has places in his heart which do not yet exist, and into them enters suffering, in order that they may have existence.

LÉON BLOY

I

A STORY HAS no beginning or end; arbitrarily one chooses that moment of experience from which to look back or from which to look ahead. I say "one chooses" with the inaccurate pride of a professional writer who—when he has been seriously noted at all—has been praised for his technical ability; but do I in fact of my own will choose that black wet January night on the Common in 1946, the sight of Henry Miles slanting across the wide river of rain, or did these images choose me? It is convenient, it is correct according to the rules of my craft, to begin just there, but if I had believed then in a God, I could also have believed in a hand plucking at my elbow, a suggestion—"Speak to him; he hasn't seen you yet."

For why should I have spoken to him? If hate is not too large a term to use in relation to any human being, I hated Henry. I hated his wife, Sarah, too. And he, I suppose, came soon after the events of that evening to hate me, as he surely at times must have hated his wife and that other, in whom in those days we were lucky enough not to believe. So this is a record of hate far more than of love, and if I come to say anything in favour of Henry and Sarah, I can be trusted. I am writing against the bias because it is my professional pride to prefer the near-truth even to the expression of my near-hate.

3

It was strange to see Henry out on such a night. He liked his comfort, and after all—or so I thought—he had Sarah. To me comfort is like the wrong memory at the wrong place or time: if one is lonely one prefers discomfort. There was too much comfort even in the bed-sitting room I had at the wrong—the south—side of the Common, in the relics of other people's furniture. I thought I would go for a walk through the rain and have a drink at the local. The little crowded hall was full of strangers' hats and coats, and I took somebody else's umbrella by accident—the man on the second floor had friends in. Then I closed the stained-glass door behind me and made my way carefully down the steps that had been blasted in 1944 and never repaired. I had reason to remember the occasion and how the stained glass, tough and ugly and Victorian, stood up to the shock as our grandfathers themselves would have done.

Directly I began to cross the Common I realized I had the wrong umbrella, for it sprang a leak, and the rain ran down under my mackintosh collar, and then it was I saw Henry. I could so easily have avoided him; he had no umbrella, and in the light of the lamp I could see his eyes were blinded with the rain. The black leafless trees gave no protection; they stood around like broken water pipes; and the rain dripped off his stiff dark hat and ran in streams down his black civil servant's overcoat. If I had walked straight by him he wouldn't have seen me, and I could have made certain by stepping two feet off the pavement, but I said, "Henry, you are almost a stranger," and saw his eyes light up as though we were old friends.

"Bendrix," he said with affection, and yet the world would have said he had the reasons for hate, not I.

"What are you up to, Henry, in the rain?" There are men whom one has an irresistible desire to tease, men whose virtues one doesn't share. He said evasively, "Oh, I wanted a bit of air," and during a sudden blast of wind and rain he just caught his hat in time from being whirled away towards the north side.

"How's Sarah?" I asked because it might have seemed odd if I hadn't, though nothing would have delighted me more than to have heard that she was sick, unhappy, dying. I imagined in those days that any suffering she underwent would lighten mine, and if she were dead I could be free: I would no longer imagine all the things one does imagine under my ignoble circumstances. I could even like poor silly Henry, I thought, if Sarah were dead.

He said, "Oh, she's out for the evening somewhere," and set that devil in my mind at work again, remembering other days when Henry must have replied just like that to other inquirers, while I alone knew where Sarah was. "A drink?" I asked, and to my surprise he put himself in step beside me. We had never before drunk together outside his home.

"It's a long time since we've seen you, Bendrix." For some reason I am a man known by his surname; I might never have been christened for all the use my friends make of the rather affected Maurice my literary parents gave me.

"A long time."

"Why, it must be—more than a year."

"June nineteen forty-four," I said.

"As long as that. Well, well." The fool, I thought, the fool to see nothing strange in a year and a half's interval. Less than five hundred yards of flat grass separated our two "sides." Had it never occurred to him to say to Sarah, "How's Bendrix doing? What about asking Bendrix in?" And hadn't her replies ever seemed to him odd, evasive, suspicious? I had fallen out of their sight as completely as a stone in a pond. I suppose the ripples may have disturbed Sarah for a week, a month; but Henry's blinkers were so firmly tied. I had hated his blinkers even when I had benefited from them, knowing that others could benefit too.

"Is she at the cinema?" I said.

"Oh, no, she hardly ever goes."

"She used to."

The Pontefract Arms was still decorated for Christmas with paper streamers and paper bills, the relics of commercial gaiety, mauve and orange, and the young landlady leaned her breasts against the bar with a look of contempt for her customers.

"Pretty," Henry said, without meaning it, and stared around with a certain lost air, a shyness, for somewhere to hang his hat. I got the impression that the nearest he had ever been before to a public bar was the chop-house off Northumberland Avenue where he ate lunch with his colleagues from the Ministry.

"What will you have?"

"I wouldn't mind a whisky."

"Nor would I, but you'll have to make do with rum."

We sat at a table and fingered our glasses; I had never had much to say to Henry. I doubt whether I should ever have troubled to know Henry or Sarah well if I had not begun in 1939 to write a story with a senior civil servant as the main character. Henry James once, in a discussion with Walter Besant, said that a young woman with sufficient talent need only pass the messroom windows of a Guards barracks and look inside in order to write a novel about the Brigade, but I think at some stage of her book she would have found it necessary to go to bed with a Guardsman if only in order to check up on the details. I didn't exactly go to bed with Henry, but I did the next best thing, and the first night I took Sarah out to dinner I had the cold-blooded intention of picking the brain of a civil servant's wife. She didn't know what I was at; she thought, I am sure, that I was genuinely interested in her family life, and perhaps that first awakened her liking for me. What time did Henry have breakfast? I asked her. Did he go to the office by tube, bus, or taxi? Did he bring his work home at night? Did he have a briefcase with the royal arms on it? Our friendship blossomed under my interest; she was so pleased that anybody should take Henry seriously. Henry was important, but important rather as an elephant is important, from the size of his department; there are some kinds of importance that remain hopelessly damned to unseriousness. Henry was an important assistant secretary in the Ministry of Pensions—later it was to be the Ministry of Home Security. Home Security—I used to laugh at that later in those moments when you hate your companion and look for any weapon. A time came when I deliberately told Sarah that I had taken Henry up only for the purposes of copy—copy too for a character who was the ridiculous, the comic element in my book. It was then she began to dislike my novel. She had an enormous loyalty to Henry —I could never deny that—and in those clouded hours when the demon took charge of my brain and I resented even harmless Henry, I would use the novel and invent episodes too crude to write. Once when Sarah had spent a whole night with me—I had looked forward to it as a writer looks forward to the last word of his book—I had spoiled the occasion suddenly by a chance word that broke the mood of what sometimes seemed for hours at a time a complete love. I had fallen sullenly asleep about two and woke at three and, putting my hand on her arm, woke Sarah. I think J had meant to make everything well again, until my victim turned her face, bleary and beautiful with sleep and full of trust, towards me. She had forgotten the quarrel, and I found even in her forgetfulness a new cause. How twisted we humans are, and yet they say a God made us; but I find it hard to conceive of any God who is not as simple as a perfect equation, as clear as air.

I said to her, "I've lain awake thinking of Chapter Five. Does Henry ever eat coffee beans to clear his breath before an important conference?" She shook her head and began to cry silently, and I of course pretended not to understand the reason—a simple question, it had been worrying me about my character, this was not an attack on Henry, the nicest people sometimes ate coffee beans. So I went on. She wept awhile and went to sleep; she was a good sleeper, and I took even her power to sleep as an added offence.

Henry drank his rum quickly, his gaze wandering mis-

erably among the mauve and orange streamers. I asked,
"Had a good Christmas?"

"Very nice. Very nice," he said.

"At home?" Henry looked up at me as though my in-
flection of the word sounded strange.

"Home? Yes, of course."

"And Sarah's well?"

"Yes."

"Have another rum?"

"It's my turn."

While Henry fetched the drinks I went into the lava-
tory. The walls were scrawled with phrases. "Damn
you, landlord, and your breasty wife." "To all pimps and
whores a merry syphilis and a happy gonorrhea." I went
quickly out again to the cheery paper streamers and the
clink of glass. Sometimes I see myself reflected too closely
in other men for comfort, and then I have an enormous
wish to believe in the saints, in heroic virtue.

I repeated to Henry the two lines I had seen. I wanted
to shock him, and it surprised me when he said simply,
"Jealousy's an awful thing."

"You mean the bit about the breasty wife?"

"Both of them. When you are miserable, you envy other
people's happiness." It wasn't what I had ever expected
him to learn in the Ministry of Home Security. And there,
in that phrase, the bitterness leaks again out of my pen.
What a dull lifeless quality this bitterness is. If I could I
would write with love, but if I could write with love I
would be another man; I would never have lost love.
Yet suddenly across the shiny tiled surface of the bar table
I felt something—nothing so extreme as love, perhaps

nothing more than a companionship in misfortune. I said to Henry, "Are *you* miserable?"

"Bendrix, I'm worried."

"Tell me."

I expect it was the rum that made him speak, or was he partly aware of how much I knew about him? Sarah was loyal, but in a relationship such as ours had been you can't help picking up a thing or two. I knew he had a mole on the left of his navel because a birthmark of my own had once reminded Sarah of it; I knew he suffered from short sight but wouldn't wear glasses with strangers (and I was still enough of a stranger never to have seen him in them); I knew his liking for tea at ten; I even knew his sleeping habits. Was he conscious that I knew so much already, so one more fact would not alter our relation? He said, "I'm worried about Sarah, Bendrix."

The door of the bar opened, and I could see the rain lashing down against the light. A little hilarious man darted in and called out, "Wotcher, everybody," and nobody answered.

"Is she ill? I thought you said—"

"No. Not ill. I don't think so." He looked miserably around; this was not his milieu. I noticed that the whites of his eyes were bloodshot; perhaps he hadn't been wearing his glasses enough, there are always so many strangers, or it might have been the after-effect of tears. He said, "Bendrix, I can't talk here," as though he had once been in the habit of talking somewhere. "Come home with me."

"Will Sarah be back?"

"I don't expect so."

I paid for the drinks, and that again was a symptom of Henry's disturbance—he never took other people's hospitality easily. He was always the one in a taxi to have the money ready in the palm of his hand, while we others fumbled.

The avenues of the Common still ran with rain, but it wasn't far to Henry's. He let himself in with a latchkey under the Queen Anne fanlight and called, "Sarah. Sarah." I longed for a reply and dreaded a reply, but nobody answered. He said, "She's out still. Come into the study."

I had never been in his study before; I had always been Sarah's friend, and when I met Henry it was on Sarah's territory—her haphazard living room where nothing matched, nothing was period or planned, where everything seemed to belong to that very week because nothing was ever allowed to remain as a token of past taste or past sentiment. Everything was used there, just as in Henry's study I now felt that very little had ever been used. I doubted whether the set of Gibbon had once been opened, and the set of Scott was only there because it had—probably—belonged to his father, like the bronze copy of the Discus Thrower. And yet he was happier in his unused room simply because it was his, his possession. I thought with bitterness and envy, if one possesses a thing securely, one need never use it.

"A whisky?" Henry said. I remembered his eyes and wondered if he were drinking more than he had done in the old days. Certainly the whiskies he poured out were generous doubles.

"What's troubling you, Henry?" I asked. I had long abandoned that novel about the senior civil servant; I wasn't looking for copy any longer.

"Sarah," he said.

Would I have been frightened if he had said that, in just that way, two years ago? No. I think I should have been overjoyed—one gets so hopelessly tired of deception. I would have welcomed the open fight if only because there might have been a chance, however small, that through some error of tactics on his side I might have won. And there has never been a time in my life before or since when I have so much wanted to win. I have never had so strong a desire even to write a good book.

He looked up at me with those red-rimmed eyes and said, "Bendrix, I'm afraid." I could no longer patronize him; he was one of misery's graduates, he had passed in the same school, and for the first time I thought of him as an equal. I remember there was one of those early brown photographs in an Oxford frame on his desk, the photograph of his father, and, looking at it, I thought how like the photograph was to Henry—it had been taken at about the same age, the middle forties—and how unlike. It wasn't the moustache that made it different; it was the Victorian look of confidence, of being at home in the world and knowing the way around, and suddenly I felt again that friendly sense of companionship. I liked him better than I would have liked his father (who had been in the Treasury). We were fellow strangers.

"What is it you're afraid of, Henry?"

He sat down in an easy chair, as though somebody had pushed him, and said with disgust, "Bendrix, I've always thought the worst thing, the very worst, a man could do—"

I should certainly have been on tenterhooks in those other days—strange to me, and how infinitely dreary, the serenity of innocence.

"You know you can trust me, Henry." It was possible, I thought, that she had kept a letter, though I had written so few. It is a professional risk that authors run. Women are apt to exaggerate the importance of their lovers and they never foresee the disappointing day when an indiscreet letter will appear marked "Interesting" in an autograph catalogue, priced at five shillings.

"Take a look at this, then," Henry said.

He held a letter out to me; it was not in my handwriting. "Go on. Read it," Henry said. It was from some friend of Henry's, and he wrote, "I suggest the man you want to help should apply to a fellow called Savage, 159 Vigo Street. I found him able and discreet, and his employees seemed less nauseous than those chaps usually are."

"I don't understand, Henry."

"I wrote to this man and said that an acquaintance of mine had asked my advice about private detective agencies. It's terrible, Bendrix. He must have seen through the pretence."

"You really mean—?"

"I haven't done anything about it, but there the letter sits on my desk, reminding me. It seems so silly, doesn't it, that I can trust her absolutely not to read it, though she comes in here a dozen times a day. I don't even put it away in a drawer. And yet I can't trust— She's out for a walk now. A *walk*, Bendrix." The rain had penetrated his guard also, and he held the edge of his sleeve towards the gas fire.

"I'm sorry."

"You were always a special friend of hers, Bendrix. They always say, don't they, that a husband is the last person really to know the kind of woman— I thought tonight when I saw you on the Common that if I told you, and you laughed at me, I might be able to burn the letter."

He sat there with his damp arm extended, looking away from me. I had never felt less like laughing, and yet I would have liked to laugh if I had been able.

I said, "It's not the sort of situation one laughs at, even if it is fantastic to think—"

He asked me longingly, "It *is* fantastic? You do think that I'm a fool, don't you?"

I would so willingly have laughed a moment before, and yet now, when I only had to lie, all the old jealousies returned. Are husband and wife so much one flesh that if one hates the wife one has to hate the husband too? His question reminded me of how easy he had been to deceive, so easy that he seemed to me almost a conniver at his wife's unfaithfulness, as the man who leaves loose banknotes in a hotel bedroom connives at theft, and I hated him for the very quality which had once helped my love.

The sleeve of his jacket steamed away in front of the gas, and he repeated, still looking away from me, "Of course, I can tell you think me a fool."

Then the demon spoke. "Oh, no, I don't think you a fool, Henry."

"You mean, you really think it's—possible?"

"Of course it's possible. Sarah's human."

He said indignantly, "And I always thought you were her friend," as though it were I who had written the letter.

"Of course," I said, "you know her so much better than I ever did."

"In some ways," he said gloomily, and I knew he was thinking of the very ways in which I had known her the best.

"You asked me, Henry, if I thought you were a fool. I only said there was nothing foolish in the idea. I said nothing against Sarah."

"I know, Bendrix. I'm sorry. I haven't been sleeping well lately. I wake up in the night, wondering what to do about this wretched letter."

"Burn it."

"I wish I could." He still had it in his hand, and for a moment I really thought he was going to set it alight.

"Or go and see Mr. Savage," I said.

"But I can't pretend to *him* that I'm not her husband. Just think, Bendrix, of sitting there in front of a desk, in a chair all the other jealous husbands have sat in, telling the same story. Do you think there's a waiting room, so that we see each other's faces as we pass through?"

Strange, I thought. You would almost have taken Henry for an imaginative man. I felt my superiority shaken, and the old desire to tease awoke in me again. I said, "Why not let me go, Henry?"

"You?" I wondered for a moment if I had gone too far, if even Henry might begin to suspect.

"Yes," I said, playing with the danger, for what did it

matter now if Henry learned a little about the past? It would be good for him and perhaps teach him to control his wife better. "I could pretend to be a jealous lover," I went on. "Jealous lovers are more respectable, less ridiculous, than jealous husbands. They are supported by the weight of literature. Betrayed lovers are tragic, never comic. Think of Troilus. I shan't lose my *amour propre* when I interview Mr. Savage." Henry's sleeve had dried, but he still held it towards the fire, and now the cloth began to scorch. He said, "Would you really do that for me, Bendrix?" And I'll swear that there were tears in his eyes, as though he had never expected or deserved this supreme mark of friendship.

"Of course I would. Your sleeve's burning, Henry."

He looked at it as though it belonged to someone else. "But this is fantastic," he said. "I don't know what I've been thinking about. First to tell you and then to ask you —this. One can't spy on one's wife through a friend— and that friend pretend to be her lover."

"Oh, it's not done," I said, "but neither is adultery or theft or running away from the enemy's fire. The not done things are done every day, Henry. It's part of modern life. I've done most of them myself."

He said, "You're a good chap, Bendrix. All I needed was a proper talk—to clear my head." And this time he really did hold the letter to the gas flame. When he had laid the last scrap in the ash tray, I said, "The name was Savage and the address either one fifty-nine or one sixty-nine Vigo Street."

"Forget it," Henry said. "Forget what I've told you.

It doesn't make sense. I've been getting bad headaches lately. I'll see a doctor."

"That was the door," I said. "Sarah's come in."

"Oh," he said, "that will be the maid. She's been to the pictures."

"No, it was Sarah's step."

He went to the door and opened it, and automatically his face fell into the absurd lines of gentleness and affection. I had always been irritated by that mechanical response to her presence because it meant nothing—one cannot always welcome a woman's presence, even if one is in love, and I believed Sarah when she told me they had never been in love. There was more genuine welcome, I believe, in my moments of hate and distrust. At least to me she was a person in her own right, not part of a home, like a bit of porcelain, to be handled with care.

"Sar-ah," he called. "Sar-ah"—spacing the syllables with an unbearable falsity.

How can I make a stranger see her as she stopped in the hall at the foot of the stairs and turned to us? I have never been able to describe even my fictitious characters except by their actions. It has always seemed to me that in a novel the reader should be allowed to imagine a character in any way he chooses; I do not want to supply him with ready-made illustrations. Now I am betrayed by my own technique, for I do not want any other woman substituted for Sarah. I want the reader to see the one broad forehead and bold mouth, the conformation of the one skull, but all I can convey is an indeterminate figure turning in a dripping mackintosh, saying, "Yes, Henry?" and then, "You?" She had always called me "you"—"Is that you?" on the telephone; "Can you? Will you? Do you?" so that I imagined, like a fool, for a few minutes at a time, that there was only one "you" in the world and that was me.

"It's nice to see you," I said. This was one of the moments of hate. "Been out for a walk?"

"Yes."

"It's a filthy night," I said accusingly, and Henry added with apparent anxiety, "You're wet through, Sarah. One day you'll catch your death of cold."

A cliché with its popular wisdom can sometimes fall through a conversation like a note of doom. yet even if we had known he spoke the truth, I wonder if either of us would have felt any genuine anxiety for her break through our own nerves, distrust, and hate.

II

I cannot say how many days passed. The old disturbance had returned, and in that state of blackness one can no more tell the days than a blind man can notice the changes of light. Was it the seventh day or the twenty-first that I decided on my course of action? I have a vague memory now, after three years have passed, of vigils along the edge of the Common, watching their house from a distance, by the pond or under the portico of the eighteenth-century church, on the off-chance that the door would open and Sarah come down those unblasted and well-scoured steps. The right hour never struck. The rainy days were over, and the nights were fine with frost, but, as in a ruined weatherhouse, neither the man nor the woman came out; never again did I see Henry making across the Common after dusk. Perhaps he was ashamed at what he had told me, for he was a very conventional man. I write the adjective with a sneer, and yet if I examine myself I find only admiration and trust for the conventional, like the villages one sees from the high-road where the cars pass, looking so peaceful in their thatch and stone, suggesting rest.

I remember I dreamed a lot of Sarah in those obscure days or weeks. Sometimes I would wake with a sense of pain, sometimes with pleasure. If a woman is in one's thoughts all day, one should not have to dream of her at night. I was trying to write a book that simply would not come. I did my daily five hundred words, but the characters never began to live. So much in writing depends on the superficiality of one's days. One may be preoccupied with shopping and income-tax returns and chance conversations, but the stream of the unconscious continues to flow undisturbed, solving problems, planning ahead; one sits down sterile and dispirited at the desk, and suddenly the words come, the situations that seemed blocked in a hopeless impasse move forward; the work has been done while one slept or shopped or talked with friends. But this hate and suspicion, love, this passion to destroy, went deeper than the book—the unconscious worked on it instead, until one morning I woke and knew, as though I had planned it overnight, that this day I was going to visit Mr. Savage.

What an odd collection the trusted professions are. One trusts one's lawyer, one's doctor, priest, I suppose, if one is a Catholic, and now I added to the list one's private detective. Henry's idea of being scrutinized by the other clients was quite wrong. The office had two waiting rooms, and I was admitted alone into one. It was curiously unlike what you would expect in Vigo Street; it had something of the musty air in the outer office of a solicitor, combined with a voguish choice of reading matter in the waiting room, which was more like a dentist's—there were *Harper's Bazaar* and *Life* and a number of French fashion periodicals—and the man who showed me in was a little too attentive and well dressed. He pulled me a chair to the fire and closed the door with great care. I felt like a patient and I suppose I was a patient, sick enough to try the famous shock treatment for jealousy.

The first thing I noticed about Mr. Savage was his tie

—I suppose it represented some old boys' association—next how well his face was shaved under the faint brush of powder, and then his forehead, where the pale hair receded, which glistened, a beacon light of understanding, sympathy, anxiety to be of service. I noticed that when he shook hands he gave my fingers an odd twist. I think he must have been a Freemason, and if I had been able to return the pressure I would probably have received special terms.

"Mr. Bendrix?" he said. "Sit down. I think that is the most comfortable chair." He patted a cushion for me and stood solicitously beside me until I had successfully lowered myself into it. Then he drew a straight chair up beside me as though he were going to listen to my pulse. "Now just tell me everything in your own words," he said—I can't imagine what other words I could have used but my own. I felt embarrassed and bitter; I had not come here for sympathy, but to pay, if I could afford it, for some practical assistance.

I began, "I don't know what your charges are for watching."

Mr. Savage gently stroked his striped tie. He said, "Don't worry about that now, Mr. Bendrix. I charge three guineas for this preliminary consultation, but if you don't wish to proceed any further I make no charge at all, none at all. The best advertisement, you know"—he slid the cliché in like a thermometer—"is a satisfied client."

In a common situation, I suppose, we all behave much alike and use the same words. I said, "This is a very simple case," and I was aware with anger that Mr. Savage really knew all about it before I began to speak. Nothing that I had to say would be strange to Mr. Savage, nothing that he could unearth would not have been dug up so many dozens of times already that year. Even a doctor is sometimes disconcerted by a patient, but Mr. Savage was a specialist who dealt in only one disease, of which he knew every symptom.

He said with a horrible gentleness, "Take your time, Mr. Bendrix."

I was becoming confused, like all his other patients. "There's really nothing to go on," I explained.

"Ah, that's my job," Mr. Savage said. "You just give me the mood, the atmosphere. I assume we are discussing Mrs. Bendrix?"

"Not exactly."

"But she passes under that name?"

"No, you are getting this quite wrong. She's the wife of a friend of mine."

"And he's sent you?"

"No."

"Perhaps you and the lady are—intimate?"

"No. I've only seen her once since nineteen forty-four."

"I'm afraid I don't quite understand. This is a watching case, you said."

I hadn't realized till then that he had angered me so much. "Can't one love or hate," I broke out at him, "as long as that? Don't make any mistake. I'm just another of your jealous clients, I don't claim to be any different from the rest, but there's been a time lag in my case."

Mr. Savage laid his hand on my sleeve as though I were a fretful child. "There's nothing discreditable about jealousy, Mr. Bendrix. I always salute it as the mark of true love. Now this lady we are discussing, you have reason to suppose that she is now—intimate with another?"

"Her husband thinks that she's deceiving him. She has private meetings. She lies about where she's been. She has—secrets."

"Ah, secrets, yes."

"There may be nothing in it, of course."

"In my long experience, Mr. Bendrix, there almost invariably is." As though he had sufficiently reassured me now to go ahead with the treatment, Mr. Savage returned to his desk and prepared to write. Name. Address. Husband's occupation. With his pencil poised for a note, Mr. Savage asked, "Does Mr. Miles know of this interview?"

"No."

"Our man mustn't be observed by Mr. Miles?"

"Certainly not."

"It adds a complication."

"I may show him your reports later. I don't know."

"Can you give me any facts about the household? Is there a maid?"

"Yes."

"Her age?"

"I wouldn't know. Thirty-eight?"

"You don't know if she has any followers?"

"No. And I don't know her grandmother's name."

Mr. Savage gave me a patient smile; I thought for a moment that he planned to leave his desk and pat me down again. "I can see, Mr. Bendrix, that you haven't had experience of inquiries. A maid's very relevant. She can tell us so much about her mistress's habits—if she is willing. You'd be surprised what a lot *is* relevant to even the simplest inquiry." He certainly that morning proved his point; he covered pages with his small scratchy handwriting. Once he broke off his questions to ask me, "Would you object, if it was urgently necessary, to my man coming to your house?" I told him I didn't mind and immediately felt as though I were admitting some infection to my own room. "If it could be avoided—"

"Of course. Of course. I understand." And I really believe he did understand. I could have told him that his man's presence would be like dust over the furniture and stain my books like soot, and he would have felt no surprise or irritation. I have a passion for writing on clean single-lined foolscap; a smear, a tea-mark on a page makes it unusable, and a fantastic notion took me that I must keep my paper locked up in case of an unsavoury visitor. I said, "It would be easier if he gave me warning."

"Certainly, but it's not always possible. Your address, Mr. Bendrix, and your telephone number?"

"It's not a private line. My landlady has an extension."

"All my men use great discretion. Would you want the reports weekly or would you prefer only to receive the finished inquiry?"

"Weekly. It may never be finished. There's probably nothing to find out."

"Have you often been to your doctor and found nothing wrong? You know, Mr. Bendrix, the fact that a man feels the need of our services almost invariably means that there is something to report."

I suppose I was lucky to have Mr. Savage to deal with. He had been recommended as being less disagreeable than men of his profession usually are, but nevertheless I found his assurance detestable. It isn't, when you come to think of it, a quite respectable trade, the detection of the innocent, for aren't lovers nearly always innocent? They have committed no crime, they are certain in their own minds that they have done no wrong, "so long as no one but myself is hurt," the old tag is ready on their lips, and love, of course, excuses everything—as they believe, and so I used to believe in the days when I loved.

And when we came to the charges, Mr. Savage was surprisingly moderate: three guineas a day, and expenses — "Which must be approved, of course." He explained them to me as "the odd coffee, you know, and sometimes our man has to stand a drink." I made a feeble joke about not approving whisky, but Mr. Savage didn't detect the humour. "I knew a case," he told me, "when a month's inquiry was saved by a double at the proper time—the cheapest whisky my client ever paid for." He explained that some of his clients liked to have a daily account, but I told him I would be satisfied with a weekly one.

The whole affair had gone very briskly; he had almost convinced me by the time I came out into Vigo Street that this was the kind of interview that happened to all men sooner or later.

III

"And if there's anything more you could tell me that would be relevant?" I remember Mr. Savage had said; a detective must find it as important as a novelist to amass his trivial material before picking out the right clue. But how difficult that picking out is—the release of the real subject. The enormous pressure of the outside world weighs on us like a *peine forte et dure*. Now that I come to write my own story the problem is still the same, but worse; there are so many more facts, now that I have not to invent them. How can I disinter the human character from the heavy scene—the daily newspaper, the daily meal, the traffic grinding towards Battersea, the gulls coming up from the Thames looking for bread, and the early summer of 1939 glinting on the park where the children sailed their boats, one of those bright condemned prewar summers? I wondered whether, if I thought long enough, I could detect, at the party Henry had given, her future lover.

We saw each other for the first time, drinking bad South African sherry because of the war in Spain. I noticed Sarah, I think, because she was happy; in those years the sense of happiness had been a long while dying under the coming storm. One detected it in drunken people, in children, seldom elsewhere. I liked her at once because she said she had read my books and left the subject there—I found myself treated at once as a human being rather than as an author. I had no idea whatever of falling in love with her. For one thing, she was beautiful, and beautiful women, especially if they are intelligent also, stir some deep feeling of inferiority in me. I don't know whether psychologists have yet named the Cophetua complex, but I have always found it hard to feel sexual desire without some sense of superiority, mental or physical. All I noticed about her that first time was her beauty and her happiness and her way of touching people with her hands, as though she loved them. I can only recall one thing she said to me, apart from that statement with which she began—"You do seem to dislike a lot of people." Perhaps I had been talking smartly about my fellow writers. I don't remember.

What a summer it was. I am not going to try to name the month exactly—I should have to go back to it through so much pain—but I remember leaving the hot and crowded room, after drinking too much bad sherry, and walking on the Common with Henry. The sun was falling flat across the Common, and the grass was pale with it. In the distance the houses were the houses in a Victorian print, small and precisely drawn and quiet; only one child cried a long way off. The eighteenth-century church stood like a toy in an island of grass—the toy could be left outside in the dark, in the dry unbreakable weather. It was the hour when you make confidences to a stranger.

Henry said, "How happy we could all be."

"Yes."

I felt an enormous liking for him, standing there on the Common, away from his own party, with tears in his eyes. I said, "You've got a lovely house."

"My wife found it."

I had met him only a week ago, at another party. He was in the Ministry of Pensions in those days, and I had buttonholed him for the sake of my material. Two days later came the card. I learned later that Sarah had got him to send it. "Have you been married long?" I asked him.

"Ten years."

"I thought your wife was charming."

"She's a great help to me," he said. Poor Henry. But why should I say poor Henry? Didn't he possess in the end the winning cards—the cards of gentleness, humility, and trust?

"I must be going back," he said. "I mustn't leave it all to her, Bendrix." And he laid his hand on my arm as though we'd known each other a year. Had he learned the gesture from her? Married people grow like each other. We walked back side by side, and as we opened the hall door I saw, reflected in a mirror from an alcove, two people separating as though from a kiss; one was Sarah. I looked at Henry. Either he had not seen or he did not care—or else, I thought, what an unhappy man he must be.

Would Mr. Savage have considered that scene relevant? It was not, I learned later, a lover who was kissing her; it was one of Henry's colleagues at the Ministry of Pensions, whose wife had run away with an able seaman a week before. Sarah had met him for the first time that day, and it seemed unlikely that he would still be part of the scene from which I had been so firmly excluded. Love doesn't take as long as that to work itself out.

I would have liked to leave that past time alone, for as

I write of 1939 I feel all my hatred returning. Hatred seems to operate the same glands as love; it even produces the same actions. If we had not been taught how to interpret the story of the Passion, would we have been able to say from their actions alone whether it was the jealous Judas or the cowardly Peter who loved Christ?

IV

When I got home from Mr. Savage's and my landlady told me that Mrs. Miles had been on the telephone, I felt the elation I used to feel when I heard the front door close and her step in the hall. I had a wild hope that the sight of me a few days before had woken not love, of course, but a sentiment, a memory which I might work on. At the time it seemed to me that if I could have her once more—however quickly and crudely and unsatisfactorily—I would be at peace again; I would have washed her out of my system, and afterwards I would leave her, not she me.

It was odd after eighteen months' silence dialling that number—Macaulay 7753—and odder still that I had to look it up in my address book because I was uncertain of the last digit. I sat listening to the ringing tone, and I wondered whether Henry was back yet from the Ministry and what I should say if he answered. Then I realized that there was nothing wrong any more with the truth. Lies had deserted me, and I felt as lonely as though they had been my only friends.

The voice of a highly trained maid repeated the number into my eardrum. I said, "Is Mrs. Miles in?"

"Mrs. Miles?"

"Isn't that Macaulay seven-seven-five-three?"

"Yes."

"I want to speak to Mrs. Miles."

"You've got the wrong number." And she rang off. It

had never occurred to me that the small things alter too with time.

I looked Miles up in the directory, but the old number was still there; the directory was more than a year out of date. I was just going to dial Inquiries when the telephone rang again, and it was Sarah herself. She said with some embarrassment, "Is that you?" She had never called me by any name and now, without her old terms of affection, she was at a loss. I said, "Bendrix speaking."

"This is Sarah. Didn't you get my message?"

"Oh, I was going to ring you, but I had to finish an article. By the way, I don't think I've got your number now. It's in the book, I suppose?"

"No. Not yet. We've changed. It's Macaulay six-two-naught-four. I wanted to ask you something."

"Yes?"

"Nothing very dreadful. I wanted to have lunch with you, that's all."

"Of course. I'd be delighted. When?"

"You couldn't manage tomorrow?"

"No. Not tomorrow. You see, I've simply got to get this article—"

"Wednesday?"

"Would Thursday do?"

"Yes," she said, and I could almost imagine disappointment in a monosyllable, so our pride deceives us.

"Then I'll meet you at the Café Royal at one."

"It's good of you," she said, and I could tell from her voice that she meant it. "Until Thursday."

"Until Thursday."

I sat with the telephone receiver in my hand and I looked at hate as at an ugly and foolish man whom one does not want to know. I dialled her number—I must have caught her before she had time to leave the phone—and said, "Sarah. Tomorrow's all right. I'd forgotten something. Same place. Same time." And, sitting there, my fingers on the quiet instrument, with something to look forward to, I thought to myself, I remember. This is what hope feels like.

V

I laid the newspaper flat on the table and read the same page over and over again because I wouldn't look at the doorway. People were continually coming in, and I wouldn't be one of those who by moving their heads up and down betray a foolish expectation. What have we all got to expect, that we allow ourselves to be so lined with disappointment? There was the usual murder in the evening paper, and a Parliamentary squabble about sweet rationing, and she was now five minutes late. It was my bad luck that she caught me looking at my watch. I heard her voice say, "I'm sorry. I came by bus, and the traffic was bad."

I said, "The tube's quicker."

"I know, but I didn't want to be quick."

She had often disconcerted me by the truth. In the days when we were in love I would try to get her to say more than the truth—that our affair would never end, that one day we should marry. I wouldn't have believed her, but I would have liked to hear the words on her tongue, perhaps only to give me the satisfaction of rejecting them myself. But she never played that game of make-believe, and then suddenly, unexpectedly, she would shatter my reserve with a statement of such sweetness and amplitude—I remember once, when I was miserable at her calm assumption that one day our relations would be over, hearing with incredulous happiness, "I have never, never loved a man as I love you, and I never shall again." Well, she hadn't known it, I thought, but she too played the same game of make-believe.

She sat down beside me and asked for a glass of lager. "I've booked a table at Rules," I said.

"Can't we stay here?"

"It's where we always used to go."

"Yes."

Perhaps we were looking strained in our manner, because I noticed we had attracted the attention of a little man who sat on a sofa not far off. I tried to outstare him, and that was easy. He had a long moustache and fawn-like eyes, and he looked hurriedly away; his elbow caught his glass of beer and spun it onto the floor, so that he was overcome with confusion. I was sorry then, because it occurred to me that he might have recognized me from my photographs; he might even be one of my few readers. He had a small boy sitting with him, and what a cruel thing it is to humiliate a father in the presence of his son. The boy blushed scarlet when the waiter hurried forward, and his father began to apologize with unnecessary vehemence.

I said to Sarah, "Of course you must lunch wherever you like."

"You see, I've never been back there."

"Well, it was never your restaurant, was it?"

"Do you go there often?"

"It's convenient for me. Two or three times a week."

She stood up abruptly and said, "Let's go"—and was suddenly taken with a fit of coughing. It seemed too big a cough for her small body; her forehead sweated with its expulsion.

"That's nasty."

"Oh, it's nothing. I'm sorry."

"Taxi?"

"I'd rather walk."

As you go up Maiden Lane, on the left-hand side there is a doorway and a grating that we passed without a word to each other. After the first dinner, when I had questioned her about Henry's habits and she had warmed to my interest, I had kissed her there rather fumblingly on the way to the tube. I don't know why I did it, unless perhaps that image in the mirror had come into my mind, for I had no intention of making love to her; I had no particular intention even of looking her up again. She was too beautiful to excite me with the idea of accessibility.

When we sat down, one of the old waiters said to me, "It's a very long time since you've been here, sir," and I wished I hadn't made my false claim to Sarah.

"Oh," I said, "I lunch upstairs nowadays."

"And you, ma'am, it's a long time too."

"Nearly two years," she said with the accuracy I sometimes hated.

"But I remember it was a big lager you used to like."

"You've got a good memory, Alfred." He beamed with pleasure at the memory. She had always had the trick of getting on well with waiters.

Food interrupted our dreary small talk, and only when we had finished the meal did she give any indication of why she was there. "I wanted you to lunch with me," she said. "I wanted to ask you about Henry."

"Henry?" I repeated, trying to keep disappointment out of my voice.

"I'm worried about him. How did you find him the other night? Was he strange at all?"

"I didn't notice anything wrong," I said.

"I wanted to ask you—oh, I know you're very busy—whether you could look him up occasionally. I think he's lonely."

"With you?"

"You know he's never really noticed me. Not for years."

"Perhaps he's begun to notice you when you aren't there."

"I'm not out much," she said, "nowadays"—and her cough conveniently broke that line of talk. By the time the fit was over she had thought out her gambits, though it wasn't like her to avoid the truth. "Are you on a new book?" she asked. It was like a stranger speaking, the kind of stranger one meets at a cocktail party. She hadn't committed that remark even the first time, over the South African sherry.

"Of course."

"I didn't like the last one much."

"It was a struggle to write at all just then. Peace coming—" and I might just as well have said, peace going.

"I sometimes was afraid you'd go back to that old idea, the one I hated. Some men would have done."

"A book takes me a year to write. It's too hard work for a revenge."

"If you knew how little you had to revenge—"

"Of course I'm joking. We had a good time together. We're adults, we knew it had to end sometime. Now, you see, we can meet like friends and talk about Henry."

I paid the bill, and we went out; and twenty yards down the street was the doorway, and the grating. I stopped on the pavement and said, "I suppose you're going to the Strand?"

"No, Leicester Square."

"I'm going to the Strand." She stood in the doorway, and the street was empty. "I'll say good-bye here. It was nice seeing you."

"Yes."

"Call me up any time you are free."

I moved towards her; I could feel the grating under my feet. "Sarah," I said. She turned her head sharply away, as though she were looking to see if anyone was coming, to see if there was time. But when she turned again the cough took her. She doubled up in the doorway and coughed and coughed. Her eyes were red with it. In her fur coat she looked like a small animal cornered.

"I'm sorry."

I said with bitterness, as though I had been robbed of something, "That needs attending to."

"It's only a cough." She held her hand out and said, "Good-bye—Maurice." The name was like an insult. I said "Good-bye," but didn't take her hand; I walked quickly away without looking round, trying to give the appearance of being busy and relieved to be gone; and when I heard the cough begin again I wished I had been able to whistle a tune, something jaunty, adventurous happy; but I have no ear for music.

VI

When young, one builds up habits of work one believes will last a lifetime and withstand any catastrophe. Over twenty years I have probably averaged five hundred words a day for five days a week. I can produce a novel in a year, and that allows time for revision and the correction of the typescript. I have always been very methodical, and when my quota of work is done I break off, even in the middle of a scene. Every now and then during the morning's work I count what I have done and mark off the hundreds on my manuscript. No printer need make a careful cast-off of my work, for there on the front page of my typescript is marked the figure—83,764. When I was young not even a love affair would alter my schedule. A love affair had to begin after lunch, and however late I might be in getting to bed—as long as I slept in my own bed—I would read the morning's work over and sleep on it. Even the war hardly affected me. A lame leg kept me out of the Army, and as I was in Civil Defence my fellow workers were only too glad that I never wanted the quiet morning turns of duty. I got, as a result, a quite false reputation for keenness, but I was keen only for my desk, my sheet of paper, that quota of words dripping slowly, methodically, from the pen. It needed Sarah to upset my self-imposed discipline. The bombs between those first daylight raids and the V-1s of 1944 kept their own convenient nocturnal habits, but so often it was only in the mornings that I could see Sarah, for in the afternoon she was never quite secure from friends, who, their shopping done, would want company and gossip before the evening siren. Sometimes she would come in between two queues, and we would make love between the greengrocer's and the butcher's.

But it was quite easy to return to work even under those conditions. As long as one is happy one can endure any discipline; it was unhappiness that broke down the habit of work. When I began to realize how often we quarrelled, how often I picked on her with nervous irritation, I became aware that our love was doomed; love had turned into a love affair with a beginning and an end. I could name the very moment when it had begun, and one day I knew I should be able to name the final hour. When she left the house I couldn't settle to work. I would reconstruct what we had said to each other; I would fan myself into anger or remorse. And all the time I knew I was forcing the pace. I was pushing, pushing the only thing I loved out of my life. As long as I could make believe that love lasted I was happy; I think I was even good to live with, and so love did last. But if love had to die, I wanted it to die quickly. It was as though our love were a small creature caught in a trap and bleeding to death; I had to shut my eyes and wring its neck.

And all that time I couldn't work. So much of a novelist's writing, as I have said, takes place in the unconscious; in those depths the last word is written before the first word appears on paper. We remember the details of our story, we do not invent them. War didn't trouble those deep sea-caves, but now there was something of infinitely greater importance to me than war, than my novel—the end of love. That was being worked out now, like a story;

the pointed word that set her crying, that seemed to have come so spontaneously to the lips, had been sharpened in those underwater caverns. My novel lagged, but my love hurried like inspiration to the end.

I don't wonder that she hadn't liked my last book. It was written all the time against the grain, without help, for no reason but that one had to go on living. The reviewers said it was the work of a craftsman—that was all that was left me of what had been a passion. I thought perhaps with the next novel the passion would return, the excitement would wake again of remembering what one had never consciously known, but for a week after lunching with Sarah at Rule's I could do no work at all. There it goes again—the I, I, I, as though this were my story, and not the story of Sarah, Henry, and, of course, that third, whom I hated without yet knowing him or even believing in him.

I had tried to work in the morning and failed; I drank too much with my lunch, so the afternoon was wasted. After dark I stood at the window with the lights turned off and could see across the flat dark Common the lit windows of the north side. It was very cold, and my gas fire warmed me only if I huddled close, and then it scorched. A few flakes of snow drifted across the lamp of the south side and touched the pane with thick damp fingers. I didn't hear the bell ring. My landlady knocked on the door and said, "A Mr. Parkis to see you," thus indicating by a grammatical article the social status of my caller. I had never heard the name, but I told her to show him in.

I wondered where I had seen before those gentle apologetic eyes, that long-outdated moustache damp with the climate. I had only turned on my reading lamp, and he came towards it, peering shortsightedly; he couldn't make me out in the shadows. He said, "Mr. Bendrix, sir?"

"Yes."

He said, "The name's Parkis," as though that might mean something to me. He added, "Mr. Savage's man, sir."

"Oh, yes. Sit down. Have a cigarette."

"Oh, no, sir," he said, "not on duty—except, of course, for purposes of concealment."

"But you aren't on duty now?"

"In a manner, sir, yes. I've just been relieved, sir, for half an hour while I make my report. Mr. Savage said as how you'd like it weekly—with expenses."

"There is something to report?" I wasn't sure whether it was disappointment I felt or excitement.

"It's not quite a blank sheet, sir," he remarked complacently, and took an extraordinary number of papers and envelopes from his pocket in searching for the right one.

"Do sit down. You make me uncomfortable."

"As you please, sir." Sitting down he could see me a little more closely. "Haven't I met you somewhere before, sir?"

I had taken the first sheet out of the envelope; it was the expense account, written in a very neat script as though by a schoolboy. I said, "You write very clearly."

"That's my boy. I'm training him in the business." He added hastily, "I don't put anything down for him, sir, unless I leave him in charge, like now."

"He's in charge, is he?"

"Only while I make my report, sir."

"How old is he?"

"Gone twelve," he said, as though his boy were a clock. "A youngster can be useful and costs nothing except a comic now and then. And nobody notices him. Boys are born lingerers."

"It seems odd work for a boy."

"Well, sir, he doesn't understand the real significance. If it came to breaking into a bedroom, I'd leave him behind."

I read:

January 18.	Two evening papers	2d.
	Tube return	1/8d.
	Coffee. Gunters	2/-

He was watching me closely as I read. "The coffee place was more expensive than I cared for," he said, "but it was the least I could take without drawing attention."

January 19.	Tubes	2/4d.
	Bottled Beers	3/-
	Cocktail	2/6d.
	Pint of bitter	1/6d.

He interrupted my reading again. "The beer's a bit on my conscience, sir, because I upset a glass owing to carelessness. But I was a little on edge, there being something to report. You know, sir, there's sometimes weeks of disappointment, but this time on the second day—"

Of course I remembered him, him and his embarrassed boy. I read under January 19 (I could see at a glance that on January 18 there was only a record of insignificant movements): "The party in question went by bus to Piccadilly Circus. She seemed agitated. She proceeded up Air Street to the Café Royal where a gentleman was waiting for her. Me and my boy—"

He wouldn't leave me alone. "You'll notice, sir, it's in a different hand. I never let my boy write the reports in case there's anything of an intimate character."

"You take good care of him," I said.

"Me and my boy sat down on a proximate couch," I read. "The party and the gentleman were obviously very close, treating each other with affectionate lack of ceremony, and I think on one occasion holding hands below the table. I could not be certain of this, but the party's left hand was out of sight and the gentleman's right hand too which generally indicates a squeeze of that kind. After a short and intimate conversation they proceeded on foot to a quiet and secluded restaurant known to its customers as Rule's and choosing a couch rather than a table they ordered two pork chops."

"Are the pork chops important?"

"They might be marks of identification, sir, if frequently indulged in."

"You didn't identify the man, then?"

"You will see, sir, if you read on."

"I drank a cocktail at the bar when I observed this

order of the pork chops, but I was unable to elicit from any of the waiters or from the lady behind the bar the identity of the gentleman. Although I couched my questions in a vague and nonchalant manner they obviously aroused curiosity, and I thought it better to leave. However by striking up an acquaintance with the stage door-keeper of the Vaudeville Theatre I was able to keep the restaurant under observation."

"How," I asked, "did you strike up the acquaintance?"

"At the bar of the Bedford Head, sir, seeing as the parties were safely occupied with the order for chops, and afterwards accompanied him back to the theatre, where the stage door—"

"I know the place."

"I have tried to compress my report, sir, to essentials."

"Quite right."

The report continued: "After lunch the parties proceeded together up Maiden Lane and parted outside a general grocery. I had the impression they were labouring under great emotion, and it occurred to me that they might be parting for good, a happy ending if I may say so to this investigation."

Again he interrupted me anxiously. "You'll forgive the personal touch?"

"Of course."

"Even in my profession, sir, we sometimes find our emotions touched, and I *liked* the lady—the party in question, that is.

"I hesitated whether to follow the gentleman or the party in question, but I decided my instructions would not permit the former. I followed the latter therefore.

She walked a little way towards Charing Cross Road, appearing much agitated. Then she turned into the National Portrait Gallery but only stayed a few minutes."

"Is there anything more of importance?"

"No, sir. I think really she was just looking for a place to sit down, because next thing she turned into a church."

"A church?"

"A Roman church, sir, in Maiden Lane. You'll find it all there. But not to pray, sir. Just to sit."

"You know even that much, do you?"

"Naturally I followed the party in. I knelt down a few pews behind so as to appear a bona fide worshipper, and I can assure you, sir, she didn't pray. She's not a Roman, is she, sir?"

"No."

"It was to sit in the dark, sir, till she calmed down."

"Perhaps she was meeting someone?"

"No, sir. She only stayed three minutes and she didn't speak to anyone. If you ask me, she wanted a good cry."

"Possibly. But you are wrong about the hands, Mr. Parkis."

"The hands, sir?"

I moved so that the light caught my face more fully. "We never so much as touched hands."

I felt sorry for him now that I had had my joke—I felt sorry to have scared yet further someone already so timid. He watched me with his mouth a little open, as though he had received a sudden hurt and was now waiting, paralysed, for the next stab. I said, "I expect that sort of mistake often happens, Mr. Parkis. Mr. Savage ought to have introduced us."

"Oh, no, sir," he said miserably, "it was up to me."
Then he bent his head and sat there, looking into his hat,
which lay on his knees. I tried to cheer him up. "It's not
serious," I said. "If you look at it from the outside, it's
really quite funny."

"But I'm on the inside, sir," he said. He turned his hat
round and went on in a voice as damp and dreary as the
Common outside. "It's not Mr. Savage I mind about, sir.
He's as understanding a man as you'll meet in the profession. It's my boy. He started with great ideas about me."
He fished from the depths of his misery a deprecating
and frightened smile. "You know the kind of reading
they do, sir. Nick Carters and the like."

"Why should he ever know about this?"

"You've got to play straight with a child, sir, and he's
sure to ask questions. He'll want to know how I followed
up; that's the thing he's learning, to follow up."

"Couldn't you tell him that I'd been able to identify the
man—just that, and I wasn't interested?"

"It's kind of you to suggest it, sir, but you have to
look at this all round. I don't say I wouldn't do it even to
my boy, but what's he going to think if he ever comes
across you in the course of the investigation?"

"That's not necessary."

"But it might well happen, sir."

"Why not leave him at home this time?"

"It's just making matters worse, sir. He hasn't got a
mother, and it's his school holidays, and I've always gone
on the lines of educating him in his holidays—with Mr.
Savage's full approval. No. I made a fool of myself that
time, and I've got to face it. If only he weren't quite so

serious, sir, but he does take it to heart when I make a floater. One day Mr. Prentice—that's Mr. Savage's assistant, a rather hard man, sir—said, 'Another of your floaters, Parkis,' in the boy's hearing. That's what opened his eyes first." He stood up with an air of enormous resolution—who are we to measure another man's courage?—and said, "I've been keeping you, sir, talking about *my* problems."

"I've enjoyed it, Mr. Parkis," I said without irony. "Try not to worry. Your boy must take after you."

"He has his mother's brains, sir," he said sadly. "I must hurry. It's cold out, though I found him a nice sheltered spot before I came away. But he's so keen   don't trust him to keep dry. Would you mind initialling the expenses, sir, if you approve them?"

I watched him from my window, with his thin mackintosh turned up and his old hat turned down; the snow had increased, and already under the third lamp he looked like a small snowman with the mud showing through. It occurred to me with amazement that for ten minutes I had not thought of Sarah or of my jealousy; I had become nearly human enough to think of another person's trouble.

VII

Jealousy, or so I have always believed, exists only with desire. The Old Testament writers were fond of using the words "a jealous God," and perhaps it was their rough and oblique way of expressing belief in the love of God for man. But I suppose there are different kinds of desire. My desire now was nearer hatred than love, and Henry, I had reason to believe from what Sarah once told me, had long ceased to feel any physical desire for her. And yet, I think, in those days he was as jealous as I was. His desire was simply for companionship. He felt for the first time excluded from Sarah's confidence; he was worried and despairing; he didn't know what was going on or what was going to happen. He was living in a terrible insecurity. To that extent his plight was worse than mine. I had the security of possessing nothing. I could have no more than I had lost, while he still owned her presence at the table, the sound of her feet on the stairs, the opening and closing of doors, the kiss on the cheek— I doubt if there was much else now, but what a lot to a starving man is just that much. And, perhaps what made it worse, he had once enjoyed the sense of security as I never had. Why, at the moment when Mr. Parkis returned across the Common, he didn't even know that Sarah and I had once been lovers. And when I write that word my brain against my will travels irresistibly back to the point where pain began.

A whole week went by after the fumbling kiss in Maiden Lane before I rang Sarah up. She had mentioned at dinner that Henry didn't like the cinema and so she rarely went. They were showing a film of one of my books at Warner's and so, partly to show off, partly because I felt that kiss must somehow be followed up for courtesy's sake, partly too because I was still interested in the married life of a civil servant, I asked Sarah to come with me. "I suppose it's no good asking Henry?"

"Not a bit," she said.

"He could join us for dinner afterwards?"

"He's bringing a lot of work back with him. Some wretched Liberal is asking a question next week in the House about widows." So you might say that the Liberal—I believe he was a Welshman called Lewis—made our bed for us that night.

The film was not a good film, and at moments it was acutely painful to see situations that had been so real to me twisted into the stock clichés of the screen. I wished I had gone to something else with Sarah. At first I had said to her, "That's not what I wrote, you know," but I couldn't keep on saying that. She touched me sympathetically with her hand, and from then on we sat there with our hands in the innocent embrace that children and lovers use. Suddenly and unexpectedly, for a few minutes only, the film came to life. I forgot that this was my story, and that for once this was my dialogue, and was genuinely moved by a small scene in a cheap restaurant. The lover had ordered steak and onions, the girl hesitated for a moment to take the onions because her husband didn't like the smell; the lover was hurt and angry because he realized what was behind her hesitation, which brought to his mind the inevitable embrace on her return home. The scene came off; I had wanted to convey the sense of passion through some common simple episode without any rhetoric in words or action, and it worked. For a few seconds I was happy. This was writing; I wasn't interested in anything else in the world. I wanted to go home and read the scene over; I wanted to work at something new; I wished, how I wished, that I hadn't invited Sarah Miles to dinner.

Afterwards—we were back at Rule's, and they had just fetched our steaks—she said, "There was one scene you did write."

"Yes."

"About the onions?"

"Yes." And at that very moment a dish of onions was put on the table. I said to her—it hadn't even crossed my mind that evening to desire her—"And does Henry mind onions?"

"Yes. He can't bear them. Do you like them?"

"Yes." She helped me to them and then helped herself.

Is it possible to fall in love over a dish of onions? It seems improbable, and yet I could swear it was just then that I fell in love. It wasn't, of course, simply the onions; it was that sudden sense of an individual woman, of a frankness that was so often later to make me happy and miserable. I put my hand under the cloth and laid it on her knee, and her hand came down and held mine in place. I said, "It's a good steak"—and heard like poetry her reply. "It's the best I've ever eaten."

There was no pursuit and no seduction. We left half the good steak on our plates and a third of the bottle of claret and came out into Maiden Lane with the same intention in both our minds. At exactly the same spot as before, by the doorway and the grill, we kissed. I said, "I'm in love."

"Me too."

"We can't go home."

"No."

We caught a taxi by Charing Cross Station, and I told the driver to take us to Arbuckle Avenue; that was the name they had given among themselves to Leinster Terrace, the row of hotels that used to stand along the side of Paddington Station, with luxury names—Ritz, Carlton, and the like. The doors of these hotels were always open, and you could get a room any time of day for an hour or two. A week ago I revisited the terrace. Half of it was gone—the half where the hotels used to stand had been blasted to bits, and the place where we made love that night was a patch of air. It had been the Bristol; there was a potted fern in the hall, and we were shown the best room by a manageress with blue hair—a real Edwardian room with a great gilt double bed and red velvet curtains and a full-length mirror (people who came to Arbuckle Avenue never required twin beds). I remember the trivial details very well: how the manageress asked me whether we wanted to stay the night; how the room cost fifteen shillings for a short stay; how the electric meter took only shillings, and we hadn't one between us; but I remember nothing else—how Sarah looked the first time, or what we did, except that we were both nervous and made love badly. It didn't matter. We had started; that was the point. There was the whole of life to look forward to then. Oh, and there's one other thing I always remember. At the door of our room ("our room" after half an hour), when I kissed her again and said how I hated the thought of her going home to Henry, she said, "Don't worry. He's busy on the widows."

"I hate even the idea of his kissing you," I said.

"He won't. There's nothing he dislikes more than onions."

I saw her home to her side of the Common. Henry's light shone below the door of his study, and we went upstairs. In the living room we held our hands against each other's bodies, unable to let go. "He'll be coming up," I said, "any moment."

"We can hear him," she said, and she added with horrifying lucidity, "There's one stair that always squeaks."

I hadn't time to take off my coat. We kissed and heard the squeak of the stair, and I watched sadly the calmness of her face when Henry came in. She said, "We were hoping you'd come up and offer us a drink."

Henry said, "Of course. What will you have, Bendrix?" I said I wouldn't have a drink; I had work to do.

"I thought you said you never worked at night."

"Oh, this doesn't count. A review."

"Interesting book?"

"Not very."

"I wish I had your power of—putting things down."

Sarah saw me to the door, and we kissed again. At that moment it was Henry I liked, not Sarah. It was as though all the men in the past and all the men in the future cast their shade over the present. "What's the matter?" she asked me. She was always quick to read the meaning behind a kiss, the whisper in the brain.

"Nothing," I said. "I'll call you in the morning."

"It would be better if I called you," she told me, and caution, I thought, caution, how well she knows how to conduct an affair like this, and I remembered again the stair that always—"always" was the word she had used —squeaked.

BOOK TWO

I

THE SENSE of unhappiness is so much easier to convey than that of happiness. In misery we seem aware of our own existence, even though it may be in the form of a monstrous egotism—this pain of mine is individual, this nerve that winces belongs to me and to no other. But happiness annihilates us; we lose our identity. The words of human love have been used by the saints to describe their vision of God; and so, I suppose, we might use the terms of prayer, meditation, contemplation to explain the intensity of the love we feel for a woman. We too surrender memory, intellect, intelligence, and we too experience the deprivation, the *noche oscura,* and sometimes as a reward a kind of peace. The act of love itself has been described as the little death, and lovers sometimes experience too the little peace. It is odd to find myself writing these phrases as though I loved what in fact I hate. Sometimes I don't recognize my own thoughts. What do I know of phrases like "the dark night" or of prayer, who have only one prayer? I have inherited them, that is all, like a husband who is left by death in the useless possession of a woman's clothes, scents, pots of cream. And yet there was this peace.

That is how I think of those first months of war—was it a phony peace as well as a phony war? It seems now to have stretched arms of comfort and reassurance all over those months of dubiety and waiting, but the peace must, I suppose, even at that time have been punctuated by misunderstanding and suspicion. Just as I went home that first evening with no exhilaration but only a sense of sadness and resignation, so again and again I returned home on other days with the certainty that I was only one of many men, the favourite lover for the moment. This woman, whom I loved so obsessively that if I woke in the night I immediately found the thought of her in my brain and abandoned sleep, seemed to give up all her time to me. And yet I could feel no trust; in the act of love I could be arrogant, but alone I had only to look in the mirror to see doubt, in the shape of a lined face and a lame leg—why me? There were always occasions when we couldn't meet—appointments with a dentist or a hairdresser, occasions when Henry entertained, when they were alone together. It was no good telling myself that in her own home she would have no opportunity to betray me (with the egotism of a lover I was already using that word with its suggestion of a nonexistent duty) while Henry worked on the widows' pensions or—for he was soon shifted from that job—on the distribution of gasmasks and the design of approved cardboard cases, for didn't I know that it was possible to make love in the most dangerous circumstances, if the desire was there? Distrust grows with a lover's success. Why, the very next time we saw each other it happened in just the way that I should have called impossible.

I woke with the sadness of her last cautious advice still resting on my mind, and within three minutes of waiting her voice on the telephone dispelled it. I have never known a woman before or since so able to alter a whole mood by simply speaking on the telephone, and when she came into a room or put her hand on my side she created at once the absolute trust I lost with every separation.

"Hullo," she said, "are you asleep?"

"No. When can I see you? This morning?"

"Henry's got a cold. He's staying at home."

"If only you could come here—"

"I've got to stay in to answer the telephone."

"Just because he's got a cold?"

Last night I had felt friendship and sympathy for Henry, but already he had become an enemy, to be mocked and resented and covertly run down.

"He's lost his voice completely."

I felt a malicious delight at the absurdity of his sickness: a civil servant without a voice, whispering hoarsely and ineffectively about widows' pensions. I said, "Isn't there any way to see you?"

"But of course."

There was silence for a moment up the phone, and I thought we had been cut off. I said, "Hullo. Hullo." But she had been thinking, that was all, carefully, collectedly, quickly, so that she could give me straight away the correct answer. "I'm giving Henry a tray in bed at one. We could have sandwiches ourselves in the living room. I'll tell him you want to talk over the film—or that story of yours." And immediately she rang off the sense of trust was disconnected, and I thought, how many times before has she planned in just this way? When I went to her house and rang the bell I felt like an enemy—or a detective, watching her words as Parkis and his son were to watch her movements a few years later. And then the door opened, and trust came back.

There was never any question in those days of who wanted whom; we were together in desire. Henry had his tray, sitting up against two pillows in his green woollen dressing-gown, and in the room below, on the hardwood floor, with a single cushion for support and the door ajar, we made love. When the moment came, I had to put my hand gently over her mouth to deaden that strange sad angry cry of abandonment, for fear Henry should hear it overhead.

To think I had intended once just to pick her brain. I crouched on the floor beside her and watched and watched, as though I might never see this again—the brown indeterminate-coloured hair like a pool of liquor on the parquet, the sweat on her forehead, the heavy breathing as though she had run a race and now like a young athlete lay in the exhaustion of victory.

And then the stair squeaked. For a moment neither of us moved. The sandwiches were stacked uneaten on the table, the glasses had not been filled. She said in a whisper, "He went downstairs." She sat in a chair, and I put a plate in her lap and a glass beside her.

"Suppose he heard," I said, "as he passed."

"He wouldn't have known what it was."

I must have looked incredulous, for she explained with dreary tenderness, "Poor Henry. It's never happened—not in the whole ten years." But all the same we weren't so sure of our safety; we sat there, silently listening, until the stair squeaked again.

My voice sounded to myself cracked and false as I said rather too loudly, "I'm glad you like that scene with the onions"; and Henry pushed open the door and looked in. He was carrying a hot-water bottle in a grey flannel cover. "Hullo, Bendrix," he whispered.

"You shouldn't have fetched that yourself," she said.

"Didn't want to disturb you."

"We were talking about the film last night."

"Hope you've got everything you want," he whispered to me. He took a look at the claret Sarah had put out for me. "Should have given him the twenty-three," he breathed in his undimensional voice and drifted out, clasping the hot-water bottle, and again we were alone.

"Do you mind?" I asked her, and she shook her head. I didn't really know what I meant; I think I had an idea that the sight of Henry might have roused remorse, but she had a wonderful way of eliminating remorse. Unlike the rest of us she was unhaunted by guilt. In her view, when a thing was done, it was done; remorse died with the act. She would have thought it unreasonable of Henry, if he had caught us, to be angry for more than a moment. Catholics are always said to be freed in the confessional from the mortmain of the past; certainly in that respect you could have called her a born Catholic, although she believed in God as little as I did—or so I thought then and wonder now.

If this book of mine fails to take a straight course, it is because I am lost in a strange region; I have no map. I sometimes wonder whether anything that I am putting down here is true. I felt that afternoon such complete trust when she said to me suddenly, without being questioned, "I've never loved anybody or anything as I do you." It was as if, sitting there in the chair with a half-eaten sandwich in her hand, she was abandoning herself as completely as she had done, five minutes back, on the hardwood floor. We most of us hesitate to make so complete a statement; we remember and we foresee and we doubt. She had no doubts. The moment only mattered. Eternity is said not to be an extension of time but an absence of time, and sometimes it seemed to me that her abandonment touched that strange mathematical point of endlessness, a point with no width, occupying no space. What did time matter—all the past and the other men she must from time to time (there is that word again) have known, or all the future in which she might be making the same statement with the same sense of truth? When I replied that I loved her too in that way, I was the liar, not she, for I never lose the consciousness of time; to me the present is never here, it is always last year or next week.

She wasn't lying even when she said, "Nobody else. Ever again." There are contradictions in time, that's all, that don't exist on the mathematical point. She had so much more capacity for love than I had. I couldn't bring down that curtain round the moment, I couldn't forget and I couldn't not fear. Even in the moment of love, I was like a police officer gathering evidence of a crime that hadn't yet been committed, and when seven years later I opened Parkis's letter the evidence was all there in my memory to add to my bitterness.

"Dear sir," the letter said, "I am glad to be able to report that me and my boy have made friendly contact with the domestic at Number 17. This has enabled the investigation to proceed with greater speed because I am sometimes able to take a squint at the party's engagement book and thus obtain movements, also inspect from day to day the contents of the party's waste-paper basket, from which I include herewith an interesting exhibit, which please return with observations. The party in question also keeps a diary and has kept one for some years, but so far the domestic who in future I shall refer to for greater security as my friend has not been able to lay hand on it, being as how the party keeps the same under lock and key, which may or may not be a suspicious circumstance. Apart from the important exhibit attached hereto, the party seems to spend a great deal of time in not keeping the appointments arranged as per her engagement book which has to be regarded as a blind, however personally unwilling to take a low view or cast a bias in an investigation of this order where exact truth is desired for the sake of all parties."

We are not hurt only by tragedy; the grotesque too carries weapons, undignified, ridiculous weapons. There were times when I wanted to crush Mr. Parkis's rambling evasive inefficient reports into his mouth in the presence of that boy of his. It was as if in my attempt to trap Sarah—but for what purpose? To hurt Henry or to hurt myself?—I had let a clown come tumbling into our intimacy. Intimacy. Even that word smacks of Mr. Parkis's reports. Didn't he write once, "Though I have no direct evidence of intimacy having taken place at 16 Cedar Road, the party certainly showed an intent to deceive."? But that was later. In this report of his I learned only that on two occasions when Sarah had written down engagements to visit her dentist and her dressmaker, she had not turned up at her appointments if they had ever existed; she had evaded pursuit. And then, turning over Mr. Parkis's crude document, written in mauve ink on cheap notepaper in his thin Waverley handwriting, I saw the bold clean writing of Sarah herself. I had not realized I would recognize it after nearly two years.

It was only a scrap of paper pinned to the back of the report, and it was marked with a big A in red pencil. Under the A, Mr. Parkis had written, "Important in view of possible proceedings that all documentary evidence should be returned for filing." The scrap had been salvaged from the waste-paper basket and smoothed carefully out as it might have been by a lover's hand. And certainly it must have been addressed to a lover: "I have no need to write to you or talk to you, you know everything before I can speak, but when one loves one feels the need to use the same old ways one has always used. I know I am only beginning to love, but already I want to abandon everything, everybody but you. Only fear and habit prevent me. Dear—"

There was no more. It stared boldly up at me, and I couldn't help thinking how I had forgotten every line of all the notes she had once addressed to me. Wouldn't

I have kept them if they had ever confessed so completely to her love, and for fear of my keeping them hadn't she always in those days been careful to write to me, as she put it, "between the lines"? But this latest love had burst the cage of lines. It had refused to be kept between them, out of sight. There was one code word I did remember—"onions." That word had been allowed in our correspondence to represent discreetly our passion. Love became "onions," even the act itself "onions." "Already I want to abandon everything, everybody but you" —and onions, I thought with hatred, onions; that was the way in my time.

I wrote "No comment" under the scrap of letter, put it in an envelope, and addressed it to Mr. Parkis; but when I woke in the night I could recite the whole thing over to myself, and the word "abandon" took on many kinds of physical image. I lay there, unable to sleep, one memory after another pricking me with hatred and desire: her hair fanning out on the parquet floor, and the stair squeaking; a day in the country when we had lain down in a ditch out of view of the road, and I could see the sparkle of frost between the fronds of hair on the hard ground, and a tractor came pushing by at the moment of crisis and the man never turned his head. Why doesn't hatred kill desire? I would have given anything to sleep. I would have behaved like a schoolboy if I had believed in the possibility of a substitute. But there was a time when I had tried to find a substitute, and it hadn't worked.

I am a jealous man—it seems stupid to write these words in what is, I suppose, a long record of jealousy:

jealousy of Henry, jealousy of Sarah, and jealousy of that other whom Mr. Parkis was so maladroitly pursuing. Now that all this belongs to the past, I feel my jealousy of Henry only when memories become particularly vivid (because I swear that if we had been married, with her loyalty and my desire, we could have been happy for a lifetime), but there still remains jealousy of my rival—a melodramatic word painfully inadequate to express the unbearable complacency, confidence, and success he always enjoys. Sometimes I think he wouldn't even recognize me as part of the picture, and I feel an enormous desire to draw attention to myself, to shout in his ear, "You can't ignore me. Here I am. Whatever happened later, Sarah loved me then."

Sarah and I used to have long arguments on jealousy. I was jealous even of the past, of which she spoke to me frankly as it came up—the affairs that meant nothing at all (except possibly the unconscious desire to find that final spasm Henry had so woefully failed to evoke). She was as loyal to her lovers as she was to Henry, but what should have provided me with some comfort—for undoubtedly she would be loyal to me too—angered me. There was a time when she would laugh at my anger, simply refusing to believe that it was genuine, just as she refused to believe in her own beauty; and I would be just as angry because she refused to be jealous of my past or my possible future. I would not believe that love could take any other form than mine; I measured love by the extent of my jealousy, and by that standard, of course, she could not love me at all.

The argument always took the same form, and I describe only one particular occasion because on that occasion the argument ended in action—a stupid action, leading nowhere, unless eventually to this doubt that always comes when I begin to write, the feeling that after all perhaps she was right and I was wrong.

I remember saying angrily, "This is just a hangover from your old frigidity. A frigid woman is never jealous; you simply haven't caught up yet on ordinary human emotions."

It angered me that she didn't make any claim. "Of course. You may be right. I'm only saying I want you to be happy. I hate your being unhappy. I don't mind anything you do that makes you happy."

"You just want an excuse. If I sleep with somebody else, you feel you can do the same—any time."

"That's neither here nor there. I want you to be happy, that's all."

"You'd make my bed for me?"

"Perhaps."

Insecurity is the worst sense that lovers feel; sometimes the most humdrum desireless marriage seems better. Insecurity twists meanings and poisons trust. In a closely beleaguered city every sentry is a potential traitor. Even before the days of Mr. Parkis I was trying to check on her; I would catch her out in small lies, evasions that meant nothing except her fear of me. For every lie I would magnify into a betrayal, and even in the most open statement I would read hidden meanings. Because I couldn't bear the thought of her so much as touching another man, I feared it all the time, and I saw intimacy in the most casual movement of the hand.

"Wouldn't you want me to be happy, rather than miserable?" she asked with unbearable logic.

"I'd rather be dead or see you dead," I said, "than with another man. I'm not eccentric. That's ordinary human love. Ask anybody. They'd all say the same—if they loved at all." I jibed at her. "Anyone who loves is jealous."

We were in my room. We had come there at a safe time of day, the late spring afternoon, in order to make love; for once we had hours of time ahead of us, and so I squandered it all in a quarrel, and there was no love to make.

She sat down on the bed and said, "I'm sorry. I didn't mean to make you angry. I expect you're right." But I wouldn't let her alone. I hated her because I wished to think she didn't love me; I wanted to get her out of my system. What grievance, I wonder now, had I got against her, whether she loved me or not? She had been loyal to me for nearly a year, she had given me a great deal of pleasure, she had put up with my moods, and what had I given her in return, apart from the momentary pleasure? I had come into this affair with my eyes open, knowing that one day this must end, and yet, when the sense of insecurity, the logical belief in the hopeless future, descended like melancholia, I would badger her and badger her, as though I wanted to bring the future in now at the door, an unwanted and premature guest. My love and fear acted like conscience. If we had believed in sin, our behaviour would hardly have differed.

"You'd be jealous of Henry," I said.

"No. I couldn't be. It's absurd."

"If you saw your marriage threatened—"

"It never would be," she said drearily, and I took her

words as an insult and walked straight out and down the stairs and into the street. Is this the end? I wondered, play-acting to myself. There's no need ever to go back. If I can get her out of my system, can't I find somewhere a quiet friendly marriage that would go on and on? Then perhaps I wouldn't feel jealous, because I wouldn't love enough, I would just be secure—and my self-pity and hatred walked hand in hand across the darkening Common like idiots without a keeper!

When I began to write I said this was a story of hatred, but I am not convinced. Perhaps my hatred is really as deficient as my love. I looked up just now from writing and caught sight of my own face in a mirror close to my desk, and I thought, does hatred really look like that? For I was reminded of that face we have all of us seen in childhood, looking back at us from the shop window, the features blurred with our breath, as we stare with such longing at the bright unobtainable objects within.

It must have been some time in May 1940 when this argument broke out. War had helped us in a good many ways, and that was how I had almost come to regard war—as a rather disreputable and unreliable accomplice in my affair. (Deliberately I would put the caustic soda of that word "affair," with its suggestion of a beginning and an end, upon my tongue.) I suppose Germany by this time had invaded the Low Countries; the spring, like a corpse, was sweet with the smell of doom, but nothing mattered to me but two practical facts: Henry had been shifted to Home Security and worked late, my landlady had removed to the basement for fear of air raids and no longer lurked upon the floor above, watching over the banisters for undesirable visitors. My own life had altered not at all, because of my lameness (I have one leg a little shorter than the other, the result of an accident in childhood); only when the air raids started did I feel it necessary to become a warden. It was for the time being as though I had signed out of the war.

That evening I was still full of my hatred and distrust when I reached Piccadilly. More than anything in the world I wanted to hurt Sarah. I wanted to take a woman back with me and lie with her upon the same bed in which I made love to Sarah; it was as though I knew that the only way to hurt her was to hurt myself. It was dark and quiet by this time in the streets, though up in the moonless sky moved the blobs and beams of the search-lights. You couldn't see faces in the side streets, where the women stood in doorways and at the entrances of the unused shelters. They had to signal with their torches like glow-worms. All the way up Sackville Street the little lights went on and off. I found myself wondering what Sarah was doing now. Had she gone home or was she waiting on the chance of my return?

A woman flashed on her light and said, "Like to come home with me, dear?" I shook my head and walked on. Farther up the street a girl was talking to a man; as she lit up her face for him, I got a glimpse of something young, dark and happy and not yet spoiled—an animal that didn't yet recognize her captivity. I passed and then came back up the road towards them; as I approached, the man left her, and I spoke. "Like a drink?" I said.

"Coming home with me afterwards?"

"Yes."

"I'll be glad of a quick one."

We went into the pub at the top of the street, and I ordered two whiskies, but as she drank I couldn't see her face for Sarah's. She was younger than Sarah—she couldn't have been more than nineteen—more beautiful, one might even have said less spoiled, but only because there was so much less to spoil. I found I no more wanted her than I wanted the company of a dog or a cat. She was telling me that she had a nice flat on the top floor only a few houses down; she told me what rent she had to pay and what her age was and where she was born, and how she had worked for a year in a café. She told me she didn't go home with anybody who spoke to her, but she could see at once I was a gentleman. She said she had a canary called Jones, named after the gentleman who had given it her. She began to talk of the difficulty of getting groundsel in London. I thought, if Sarah is still in my room I can ring up. I heard the girl asking me whether if I had a garden I would sometimes remember her canary. She said, "You don't mind me asking, do you?"

Looking at her over my whisky, I thought how odd it was that I felt no desire for her at all. It was as if quite suddenly, after all the promiscuous years, I had grown up. My passion for Sarah had killed simple lust forever. Never again would I be able to enjoy a woman without love.

And yet surely it was not love that had brought me into this pub; I had told myself all the way from the Common that it was hate—as I tell myself still, writing this account of her, trying to get her out of my system forever, for I have always told myself that if she died I could forget her.

I went out of the pub, leaving the girl with her whisky to finish and a pound note as a salve to her pride, and walked up New Burlington Street as far as a telephone box. I had no torch with me and I was forced to strike match after match before I could complete the dialling of my number. Then I heard the ringing tone, and I could imagine the telephone where it stood on my desk, and I knew exactly how many steps Sarah would have to take to reach it if she were sitting in a chair or lying on the bed. And yet I let it go on ringing in the empty room for half a minute. Then I telephoned to her home, and the maid told me she had not yet come in. I thought of her walking about on the Common in the blackout—it wasn't a very safe place in those days—and, looking at my watch, I thought, if I hadn't been a fool we should still have had three hours together. I went back home alone and tried to read a book, but all the time I was listening for the telephone, which never rang. My pride prevented me from telephoning her again. At last I went to bed and took a double dose of sleeping draught, so that the first I knew in the morning was Sarah's voice on the telephone, speaking to me as if nothing had happened. It was like perfect peace again until I put the receiver down, when immediately that devil in my brain prompted the thought that the waste of those three hours meant nothing at all to her.

I have never understood why people who can swallow the enormous improbability of a personal God boggle at a personal devil. I have known so intimately the way that

demon works in my imagination. No statement that
Sarah ever made was proof against his cunning doubts,
though he would usually wait till she had gone to utter
them. He would prompt our quarrels long before they
occurred; he was not Sarah's enemy so much as the enemy of love, and isn't that what the devil is supposed to
be? I can imagine that if there existed a God who loved,
the devil would be driven to destroy even the weakest,
the most faulty imitation of that love. Wouldn't he be
afraid that the habit of love might grow, and wouldn't he
try to trap us all into being traitors, into helping him ex-
tinguish love? If there is a God who uses us and makes
his saints out of such material as we are, the devil too
may have his ambitions; he may dream of training
even such a person as myself, even poor Parkis, into being
his saints, ready with borrowed fanaticism to destroy
love wherever we find it.

III

For I thought I could detect in Parkis's next report a genuine enthusiasm for the devil's game. At last he had really scented love and now he stalked it, his boy at his heels like a retriever. He had discovered where Sarah was spending so much of her time; more than that, he knew for certain that the visits were surreptitious. I had to admit that Mr. Parkis had proved himself an astute detective. He had arranged, with the help of his boy, to get the Miles maid outside the house just at the moment when the "party in question" walked down Cedar Road towards Number 16. Sarah stopped and spoke to the maid, whose day off it was, and the maid introduced her to young Parkis. Then Sarah went on and turned the next corner, where Parkis himself was waiting. He saw her walk a little way and then return. When she found that the maid and young Parkis were out of sight she rang the bell at Number 16. Mr. Parkis then set to work to check on the inhabitants of Number 16. This was not so easy, as the house was divided into flats, and he had no means yet of knowing which of the three bells Sarah had rung. He promised a final report in a few days. All he had to do, when next Sarah started out in this direction, was to get ahead of her and dust the three bells with powder. "There is of course, apart from exhibit A, no proof of misconduct by the party in question. If on the strength of these reports such proofs are required with a view to legal proceedings, it may be necessary after a suitable interval to follow the party into the flat. A second witness, who can identify the party, would be required. It is not necessary to catch the party in the act; a certain disarrangement of clothes and agitation might be held sufficient by the courts."

Hatred is very like physical love; it has its crisis and then its period of calm. Poor Sarah, I could think, reading Mr. Parkis's report, for this moment had been the orgasm of my hatred, and now I was satisfied. I could feel sorry for her, hemmed in as she was. She had committed nothing but love, and here were Parkis and his boy, watching every movement, plotting with her maid, putting powder on bells, planning violent eruptions into what perhaps was the only peace that nowadays she enjoyed. I had half a mind to tear up the report and call the spies off her. Perhaps I would have done so if I had not, at the seedy literary club to which I belonged, opened a *Tatler* and seen Henry's photograph. Henry was successful now; in the last Birthday Honours he had received a C.B.E. for his services at the Ministry; he had been appointed Chairman of a Royal Commission; and here he was at the gala night of a British film called *The Last Siren*, pallid and pop-eyed in the flashlight, with Sarah on his arm. She had lowered her head to escape the flash, but I would have recognized that close knotty hair which trapped or resisted the fingers. Suddenly I wanted to put out my hand and touch her, the hair of her head and her secret hair; I wanted her lying beside me, I wanted to be able to turn my head on the pillow and speak to her, I wanted the almost imperceptible smell and taste of her skin; and there was Henry, facing the pressman's camera with the complacency and assurance of a departmental head.

I sat down under a staghead presented by Sir Walter Besant in 1898 and wrote to Henry. I wrote that I had something of importance to discuss with him and would he lunch with me—he could choose any day during the next week. It was typical of Henry that he rang up with great promptitude and at the same time suggested I should lunch with him; never have I known a man who was a more uneasy guest. I can't remember exactly what the excuse was, but it angered me. I think he said his own club had some particularly good port, but the real reason was that the sense of obligation irked him—even the small obligation of a free meal. He little guessed how small his obligation was going to be. He had chosen a Saturday, and on that day my club is almost empty. The daily journalists have no paper to produce; the school inspectors have gone home to Bromley and Streatham; I never know quite what happens on that day to the clergy —perhaps they stay indoors to prepare their sermons. As for the authors—for whom the club had been founded— nearly all of them are hanging on the wall: Conan Doyle, Charles Garvice, Stanley Weyman, Nat Gould, with an occasional more illustrious and familiar face; the living you can count on the fingers of one hand. I have always felt at home in the club because there is so little likelihood of meeting a fellow writer.

I remember Henry chose a Vienna steak; it was a mark of his innocence. I really believe that he had no idea what he was ordering and expected something like a

Wiener Schnitzel. Playing as he was away from the home ground, he was too ill at ease to comment on the dish, and somehow he managed to ram the pink soggy mixture down. I remembered that pompous appearance before the flashlights and made no attempt to warn him when he chose Cabinet Pudding. During the hideous meal (the club that day surpassed itself) we talked elaborately about nothing. Henry did his best to lend an appearance of Cabinet secrecy to the proceedings of a Royal Commission that were reported daily in the press. We went into the lounge for coffee and found ourselves entirely alone beside the fire in a waste of black horsehair sofas. I thought how suitable the horns along the walls were to the situation and, putting my feet up on the old-fashioned fender, shut Henry firmly into his corner. I stirred my coffee and said, "How's Sarah?"

"Pretty well," Henry said evasively. He tasted his port with care and suspicion; he hadn't forgotten, I suppose, the Vienna steak.

"Are you still worried?" I asked him.

He shifted his gaze unhappily. "Worried?"

"You *were* worried. You told me so."

"I don't remember. She's pretty well," he explained weakly, as though I had been referring to her health.

"Did you ever consult that detective?"

"I hoped you'd forgotten it. I wasn't well—you see there was this Royal Commission brewing. I was overworked."

"Do you remember I offered to see him for you?"

"We must both have been a bit overwrought." He stared up at the old horns overhead, screwing up his eyes in his attempt to read the name of the donor. He said stupidly, "You seem to have a lot of heads."

I wasn't going to let him off. I said, "I went to see him a few days later."

He put down his glass and said, "Bendrix, you had absolutely no right—"

"I'm paying all the charges."

"It's infernal cheek." He stood up, but I had him penned in where he couldn't get past without an act of violence, and violence wasn't in Henry's character.

"Surely you'd have liked her cleared?" I said.

"There was nothing to clear. I want to go, please."

"I think you ought to read the reports."

"I've no intention—"

"Then I think I shall have to read you the bit about the surreptitious visits. Her love letter I returned to the detectives for filing. My dear Henry, you've been properly led up the garden."

I really thought that he was going to hit me. If he had, I would have struck back with such pleasure, struck back at this oaf to whom Sarah had remained in her way so stupidly loyal for so many years; but at that moment the secretary of the club came in. He was a man with a long grey beard and a soup-stained waistcoat, who looked like a Victorian poet but in fact wrote little sad reminiscences of the dogs he had once known (*Forever Fido* had been a great success in 1912). "Ah, Bendrix," he said, "I haven't seen you here in a long while." I introduced him to Henry, and he said with the quickness of a hairdresser, "I've been following the reports every day."

"What reports?" For once Henry's work had not come first to his mind when that word was uttered.

"The Royal Commission."

When at last he had gone Henry said, "Now will you please give me the reports and let me pass."

I imagined that he had been thinking things over while the secretary was with us, so I handed him the last report. He put it straight into the fire and rammed it home with the poker. I couldn't help thinking that the gesture had dignity. "What are you going to do?" I asked.

"Nothing."

"You haven't got rid of the facts."

"To hell with the facts," Henry said. I had never heard him swear before.

"I can always let you have a carbon copy."

"Will you let me go now?" Henry said. The demon had done its work, the orgasm was over, I felt drained of venom. I took my legs off the fender and let Henry pass. He walked straight out of the club, forgetting his hat, that black superior hat that I had seen come dripping across the Common—it seemed an age and not a matter of weeks ago.

IV

I had expected to overtake him, or at least to come in sight of him ahead up the long reach of Whitehall, and so I carried his hat with me, but he was nowhere to be seen. I turned back, not knowing where to go. That is the worst of time nowadays; there is so much of it. I looked in the small bookshop near Charing Cross Underground and wondered whether Sarah at this moment might have laid her hand on the powdered bell in Cedar Road with Mr. Parkis waiting round the corner. If I could have turned back time I think I would have done so; I would have let Henry go walking by, blinded by the rain. But I am beginning to doubt whether anything I can do will ever alter the course of events. Henry and I are allies now, in our fashion, but are we allies against an infinite tide?

I went across the road, past the fruit hawkers, and into the Victoria Gardens. Not many people were sitting on the benches in the grey windy air, and almost at once I saw Henry, but it took me a moment to recognize him. Out of doors, without a hat, he seemed to have joined the anonymous and the dispossessed, the people who come up from the poorer suburbs and whom nobody knows— the old man feeding sparrows, the woman with a brown paper parcel marked Swan & Edgars. He sat there with his head bent, looking at his shoes. I had been sorry for myself for so long, so exclusively, that it seemed strange to me to feel sorry for my enemy. I put the hat quietly down on the seat beside him and would have walked away, but he looked up and I could see that he had been crying. He must have travelled a very long way. Tears belong to a different world from Royal Commissions.

"I'm sorry, Henry," I said. How easily we believe we can slide out of our guilt by a motion of contrition.

"Sit down," Henry commanded with the authority of his tears, and I obeyed him. He said, "I've been thinking. Were you two lovers, Bendrix?"

"Why should you imagine—"

"It's the only explanation."

"I don't know what you are talking about."

"It's the only excuse too, Bendrix. Can't you see that what you've done is—monstrous?" As he spoke he turned his hat over and checked the maker's name.

"I suppose you think I'm an awful fool, Bendrix, not to have guessed. Why didn't she leave me?"

Had I got to instruct him about the character of his own wife? The poison was beginning to work in me again. I said, "You have a good safe income. You're a habit she's formed. You're security." He listened seriously and attentively as though I were a witness before the Commission, giving evidence on oath. I went sourly on. "You were no more trouble to us than you'd been to the others."

"There were others too?"

"Sometimes I thought you knew all about it and didn't care. Sometimes I longed to have it out with you— like we are doing now, when it's too late. I wanted to tell you what I thought of you."

"What did you think?"

"That you were her pimp. You pimped for me and

you pimped for them, and now you are pimping for the latest one. The eternal pimp. Why don't you get angry, Henry?"

"I never knew."

"You pimped with your ignorance. You pimped by never learning how to make love with her, so she had to look elsewhere. You pimped by giving opportunities. You pimped by being a bore and a fool, so now somebody who isn't a bore and a fool is playing about with her in Cedar Road."

"Why did she leave you?"

"Because I became a bore and a fool too. But I wasn't born one, Henry. You created me. She wouldn't leave you, so I became a bore, boring her with complaints and jealousy."

He said, "People have a great opinion of your books."

"And they say you're a first-class chairman. What the hell does our work matter?"

He said sadly, "I don't know anything else that does," looking up at the grey cumulus passing above the south bank. The gulls flew low over the barges, and the shot tower stood black in the winter light among the ruined warehouses. The man who fed the sparrows had gone, and the woman with the brown paper parcel; the fruit sellers cried like animals in the dusk outside the station. It was as if the shutters were going up on the whole world; soon we would all of us be abandoned to our own devices. "I wondered why you hadn't been to see us all that time," Henry said.

"I suppose, in a way, we'd got to the end of love. There was nothing else we could do together. She could shop and cook and fall asleep with you, but she could only make love with me."

"She's very fond of you," he said, as though it were his job to comfort me, as though my eyes were the ones bruised with tears.

"One isn't satisfied with fondness."

"I was."

"I wanted love to go on and on, never to get less." I had never spoken to anyone like this, except Sarah, but Henry's reply was not Sarah's. He said, "It's not in human nature. One has to be satisfied." But that wasn't what Sarah had said, and, sitting there beside Henry in the Victoria Gardens, watching the day die, I remembered the end of the whole affair.

She had said to me—they were nearly the last words I heard from her before she came dripping into the hall from her assignation—"You needn't be so scared. Love doesn't end. Just because we don't see each other . . ." She had already made her decision, though I didn't know it till next day, when the telephone presented nothing but the silent open mouth of somebody found dead. She said, "My dear, my dear. People go on loving God, don't they, all their lives, without seeing him?"

"That's not our kind of love."

"I sometimes don't believe there's any other kind." I suppose I should have recognized that she was already under a stranger's influence; she had never spoken like that when we were first together. We had agreed so happily to eliminate God from our world. As I shone the torch carefully to light her way across the devastated hall, she said again, "Everything must be all right. If we love enough."

"I can't turn on any more," I said. "You've got everything."

"You don't know," she said. "You don't know."

The glass from the windows crumbled under our feet. Only the old Victorian stained glass above the door had stood firm. The glass turned white where it powdered, like the ice children have broken in wet fields or along the sides of roads. She told me again, "Don't be scared." I knew she wasn't referring to these strange new weapons that still after five hours droned steadily up from the south like bees.

It was the first night of what were later called the V-1s, in June 1944. We had become unused to air raids. Apart from the short spell in February 1944, there had been nothing since the blitz petered out with the great final raids of 1941. When the sirens went and the first robots came over, we assumed that a few planes had broken through our night defence. One felt a sense of grievance when the All Clear had still not sounded after an hour. I remember saying to Sarah, "They must have got slack. Too little to do." And at that moment, lying in the dark on my bed, we saw our first robot. It passed low across the Common, and we took it for a plane on fire and its odd deep bumble for the sound of an engine out of control. A second came, and then a third. We changed our minds then about our defences. "They are shooting them like pigeons," I said. "They must be crazy to go on." But go on they did, hour after hour, even after the dawn had begun to break, until even we realized that this was something new.

We had only just lain down on the bed when the raid started. It made no difference. Death never mattered at those times; in the early days I even used to pray for it: the shattering annihilation that would prevent forever the getting up, the putting on of clothes, the watching her torch trail across to the opposite side of the Common like the tail light of a slow car driving away. I have wondered sometimes whether eternity might not after all exist as the endless prolongation of the moment of death, and that was the moment I would have chosen, that I would still choose if she were alive, the moment of absolute trust and absolute pleasure, the moment when it was impossible to quarrel because it was impossible to think. I have complained of her caution and bitterly compared our use of the word "onions" with the scrap of her writing Mr. Parkis had salvaged, but reading her message to my unknown successor would have hurt less if I hadn't known how capable she was of abandonment.

No, the V-1s didn't affect us until the act of love was over. I had spent everything I had and was lying back with my head on her stomach and her taste—as thin and elusive as water—in my mouth, when one of the robots crashed down onto the Common, and we could hear the glass breaking farther down the south side.

"I suppose we ought to go to the basement," I said.

"Your landlady will be there. I can't face other people."

After possession comes the tenderness of responsibility, when one forgets one is only a lover, responsible for nothing. I said, "She may be away. I'll go down and see."

"Don' go. Please don't go."

"I won't be a moment." It was a phrase one continued to use, although one knew in those days that a moment might well be eternity-long. I put on my dressing-gown and found my torch. I hardly needed it; the sky was grey now, and in the unlit room I could see the outline of her face.

She said, "Be quick."

As I ran down the stairs I heard the next robot coming over, and then the sudden waiting silence when the engine cut out. We hadn't yet had time to learn that that was the moment of risk, to get out of the line of glass, to lie flat. I never heard the explosion, and I woke after five seconds or five minutes in a changed world. I thought I was still on my feet and I was puzzled by the darkness; somebody seemed to be pressing a cold fist into my cheek, and my mouth was salty with blood. My mind for a few moments was clear of everything except a sense of tiredness as though I had been on a long journey. I had no memory at all of Sarah and I was completely free from anxiety, jealousy, insecurity, hate; my mind was a blank sheet on which somebody had just been on the point of writing a message of happiness. I felt sure that when my memory came back the writing would continue, and that I should be happy.

But when memory did return it was not in that way. I realized first that I was lying on my back and that what balanced over me, shutting out the light, was the front door; some other debris had caught it and suspended it a few inches above my body, though the odd thing was that later I found myself bruised from the shoulders to the knees as if by its shadow. The fist that fitted into my cheek was the china handle of the door, and it had knocked out a couple of my teeth. After that, of course, I remembered Sarah and Henry and the dread of love ending.

I got out from under the door and dusted myself down. I called to the basement, but there was nobody there. Through the blasted doorway I could see the grey morning light, and I had a sense of great emptiness stretching out from the ruined hall; I realized that a tree which had blocked the light had simply ceased to exist; there was no sign of even a fallen trunk. A long way off wardens were blowing whistles. I went upstairs. The first flight had lost its banisters and was a foot deep in plaster, but the house hadn't really, by the standard of those days, suffered badly; it was our neighbours who had caught the full blast. The door of my room was open, and, coming along the passage, I could see Sarah; she had got off the bed and was crouched on the floor—from fear, I supposed. She looked absurdly young, like a naked child. I said, "That was a close one."

She turned quickly and stared at me with fear. I hadn't realized that my dressing-gown was torn and dusted all over with plaster; my hair was white with it, and there was blood on my mouth and cheeks. "Oh, God," she said, "you're alive."

"You sound disappointed."

She got up from the floor and reached for her clothes. I told her, "There's no point in your going yet. There must be an All Clear soon."

"I've got to go," she said.

"Two bombs don't fall in one place," I said, but automatically, for that was a piece of folklore that had often proved false.

"You're hurt."

"I've lost two teeth, that's all."

"Come over here, let me wash your face." She had finished dressing before I had time to make another protest; no woman I have ever known could dress so quickly. She bathed my face very slowly and carefully.

"What were you doing on the floor?" I asked.

"Praying."

"Who to?"

"To anything that might exist."

"It would have been more practical to come down-stairs." Her seriousness frightened me. I wanted to tease her out of it.

"I did," she said.

"I didn't hear you."

"There was nobody there. I couldn't see you, until I saw your arm stretching out from under the door. I thought you were dead."

"You might have come and tried."

"I did. I couldn't lift the door."

"There was room to move me. The door wasn't hold-ing me. I'd have woken up."

"I don't understand. I knew for certain you were dead."

"There wasn't much to pray for, then, was there?" I teased her. "Except a miracle."

"When you are hopeless enough," she said, "you can pray for miracles. They happen, don't they, to the poor, and I was poor."

"Stay till the All Clear." She shook her head and walked straight out of the room. I followed her down the stairs and began against my will to badger her. "Shall I see you this afternoon?"

"No. I can't."

"Some time tomorrow—"

"Henry's coming back."

Henry. Henry. Henry. That name tolled through our

relationship, damping every mood of happiness or fun or exhilaration with its reminder that love dies, affection and habit win the day. "You needn't be so scared," she said. "Love doesn't end. . . ." And nearly two years passed before that meeting in the hall and, "You?"

VI

For days after that, of course, I had hope. It was only a coincidence, I thought, that the telephone wasn't answered, and when after a week I met the maid and inquired about the Mileses and learned that Sarah was away in the country, I told myself that in wartime letters are lost. Morning after morning I would hear the rattle in the postbox and deliberately I would remain upstairs until my landlady fetched my mail. I wouldn't look through the letters—disappointment had to be postponed, hope kept alive as long as possible. I would read each letter in turn, and only when I reached the bottom of the pile could I be certain that there was nothing from Sarah. Then life withered until the four-o'clock post, and after that one had to get through the night again.

For nearly a week I didn't write to her; pride prevented me, until one morning I abandoned it completely, writing anxiously and bitterly, marking the envelope, addressed to the north side, "Urgent" and "Please forward." I got no reply and then I gave up hope and remembered exactly what she had said. "People go on loving God, don't they, all their lives without seeing him?" I thought with hatred, she always has to show up well in her own mirror; she mixes religion with desertion to make it sound noble to herself. She won't admit that now she prefers to go to bed with X.

That was the worst period of all. It is my profession to imagine, to think in images; fifty times through the day, and immediately I woke during the night, a curtain would rise and the play would begin—always the same play: Sarah making love, Sarah with X, doing the same things that we had done together, Sarah kissing in her own particular way, arching herself in the act of sex and uttering that cry like pain, Sarah in abandonment. I would take pills at night to make me sleep quickly, but I never found any pills that would keep me asleep till daylight. Only the robots were a distraction during the day; for a few seconds between the silence and the crash my mind would be clear of Sarah. Three weeks passed, and the images were as clear and frequent as at first, and there seemed no reason why they should ever end, and I began quite seriously to think of suicide. I even set a date and I saved up my sleeping pills with what was almost a sense of hope. I needn't after all go on like this indefinitely, I told myself. Then the date came, and the play went on and on, and I didn't kill myself. It wasn't cowardice; it was a memory that stopped me—the memory of the look of disappointment on Sarah's face when I came into the room after the V-1 had fallen. Hadn't she, at heart, hoped for my death, so that her new affair with X would hurt her conscience less—for she had a kind of elementary conscience? If I killed myself now, she wouldn't have to worry about me at all, and surely after four years together there would be moments of worry even with X. I wasn't going to give her that satisfaction. If I had known a way, I would have increased her worries to breaking point, and my inability to do so angered me. How I hated her.

Of course there is an end of hate as there is an end of love. After six months I realized that I had not thought of Sarah all one day and that I had been happy. It couldn't have been quite the end of hate because at once I went into a stationer's to buy a picture postcard and write a jubilant message on it that might—who knows? —cause a momentary pain, but by the time I had written her address I had lost the desire to hurt and dropped the card into the road. It was strange that hate should have been revived again by that meeting with Henry. I remember thinking, as I opened Mr. Parkis's next report, if only love could revive like that too.

Mr. Parkis had done his work well: the powder had worked, and the flat had been located—the top flat in 16 Cedar Road; the occupants, a Miss Smythe and her brother, Richard. I wondered whether Miss Smythe was as convenient a sister as Henry was a husband, and all my latent snobbery was aroused by the name—that y, the final e. I thought, has she fallen as low as a Smythe in Cedar Road? Was he the end of a long chain of lovers in the last two years, or when I saw him—and I was determined to see him less obscurely than in Mr. Parkis's reports—would I be looking at the man for whom she had deserted me in June 1944?

"Shall I ring the bell and walk right in and confront him like an injured husband?" I asked Mr. Parkis, who had met me by appointment in an A.B.C.—it was his own suggestion, as he had the boy with him and couldn't take him into a bar.

"I'm against it, sir," Mr. Parkis said, adding a third spoonful of sugar to his tea. His son sat at a table out of earshot with a glass of orangeade and a bun. He observed everybody who came in, as they shook the thin watery snow from their hats and coats, watched with his alert brown beady eyes as though he had to make a report later —perhaps he had, part of the Parkis training. "You see, sir," Mr. Parkis said, "unless you were willing to give evidence, it complicates things in the courts."

"It will never reach the courts."

"An amicable settlement?"

"A lack of interest," I said. "One can't really make a fuss about a man called Smythe. I'd just like to see him, that's all."

"The safest thing, sir, would be a meter inspector."

"I can't dress up in a peaked cap."

"I share your feelings, sir. It's a thing I try to avoid. And I'd like the boy to avoid it too, when the time comes." His sad eyes followed every movement his boy made. "He wanted an ice, sir, but I said no, not in this weather." And he shivered a little, as though the thought of the ice had chilled him. For a moment I had no idea of his meaning when he said, "Every profession has its dignity, sir."

I said, "Would you lend me your boy?"

"If you assure me there'll be nothing unpleasant, sir," he said doubtfully.

"I don't want to call when Mrs. Miles is there. This scene will have a Universal certificate."

"But why the boy, sir?"

"I'll say he's feeling ill. We've come to the wrong address. They couldn't help letting him sit down for a while."

"It's in the boy's capacity," Mr. Parkis said with pride, "and nobody can resist Lance."

"He's called Lance, is he?"

"After Sir Lancelot, sir. Of the Round Table."

"I'm surprised. That was a rather unpleasant episode, surely."

"He found the Holy Grail," Mr. Parkis said.

"That was Galahad. Lancelot was found in bed with Guinevere."

Why do we have this desire to tease the innocent? Is it envy? Mr. Parkis said sadly, looking across at his boy as though he had betrayed him, "I hadn't heard."

VII

Next day—to spite his father—I gave the boy an ice in the High Street before we went to Cedar Road. Henry Miles was holding a cocktail party, so Mr. Parkis had reported, and the coast was clear. He handed the boy over to me, after twitching his clothes straight. The boy was wearing his best things in honour of his first stage appearance with a client, while I was wearing my worst. The effect was rather like Little Lord Fauntleroy out with a groom. Some of the strawberry ice fell from his spoon and made a splash upon his suit. I sat in silence till the last drop was drained. Then I said, "Another?" He nodded. "Strawberry again?"

He said, "Vanilla"—and added a long while after, "Please."

He ate the second ice with great deliberation, carefully licking the spoon as though he were removing fingerprints. Then we went hand in hand across the Common to Cedar Road, like a father and son. Sarah and I are both childless, I thought. Wouldn't there have been more sense in marrying and having children and living quietly together in a sweet and dull peace than in this furtive business of lust and jealousy and the reports of Parkis?

I rang the bell on the top floor of Cedar Road. I said to the boy, "Remember. You're feeling ill."

"If they give me an ice—" he began. Parkis had trained him to be prepared.

"They won't."

I assumed it was Miss Smythe who opened the door—

a middle-aged woman with the grey tired hair of charity bazaars. I said, "Does Mr. Wilcox live here?"

"No. I'm afraid—"

"You don't happen to know if he's in the flat below?"

"There's nobody called Wilcox in this house."

"Oh, dear," I said. "I've brought the boy all this way, and now he's feeling ill."

I dared not look at the boy, but, from the way in which Miss Smythe gazed at him, I felt sure he was silently and efficiently carrying out his part; Mr. Savage would have been proud to acknowledge him as a member of his team.

"Do let him come in and sit down," Miss Smythe said.

"It's very kind of you."

I wondered how often Sarah had passed through this door into the little cluttered hall. Here I was, in the home of X. Presumably the brown soft hat on the hook belonged to him. The fingers of my successor—the fingers that touched Sarah—daily turned the handle of this door which opened now on the yellow flame of the gas fire, pink-shaded lamps burning through the snow-grey afternoon, a waste of cretonne loose covers. "Can I fetch your little boy a glass of water?"

"It's very kind of you." I remembered I had said that before.

"Or some orange squash?"

"You mustn't bother."

"Orange squash," the boy said firmly. Again the long pause and, "Please," as she went through the door. Now we were alone I looked at him; he really did look ill, crouching back on the cretonne. If he had not winked at me I would have wondered whether perhaps— Miss

Smythe returned, carrying the orange squash, and I said, "Say thank you, Arthur."

"Is his name Arthur?"

"Arthur James," I said.

"It's quite an old-fashioned name."

"We're an old-fashioned family. His mother was fond of Tennyson."

"She's—?"

"Yes," I said, and she looked at the child with commiseration.

"He must be a comfort to you."

"And an anxiety," I said. I began to feel shame; she was so unsuspicious, and what good was I doing here? I was no nearer meeting X, and would I be any happier for giving a face to the man upon the bed? I altered my tactics. I said, "I ought to introduce myself. My name is Bridges."

"And mine is Smythe."

"I have a strong feeling I have met you somewhere before."

"I don't think so. I have a very good memory for faces."

"Perhaps I have seen you on the Common."

"I go there sometimes with my brother."

"Not by any chance a John Smythe?"

"No," she said, "Richard. How is the little boy feeling?"

"Worse," said Parkis's son.

"Do you think we ought to take his temperature?"

"Can I have some more orange squash?"

"It can do no harm, can it?" Miss Smythe wondered. "Poor child!"

"We've trespassed on you enough."

"My brother would never forgive me if I didn't make you stay. He's very fond of children."

"Is your brother in?"

"I'm expecting him any moment."

"Home from work?"

"Well, his working day is really Sunday."

"A clergyman?" I asked with secret malice and received the puzzling answer, "Not exactly." A look of worry came down like a curtain between us, and she retired behind it with her private troubles. As she got up, the hall door opened, and there was X. I had an impression, in the dusk of the hall, of a man with a handsome actor's face—a face that looked at itself too often in mirrors, a taint of vulgarity; and I thought sadly and without satisfaction, I wish she had better taste. Then he came through into the light of the lamps, and the purple crumpled strawberry mark stretching from above the cheekbone down to the point of the chin was almost like a mark of distinction. I had maligned him; he could have no satisfaction in looking at that.

Miss Smythe said, "My brother, Richard. Mr. Bridges. Mr. Bridges' little boy is not feeling well. I asked them in."

He shook hands, his eye on the boy; I noticed the dryness and heat of his hands. He said, "I've seen your boy before."

"On the Common?"

"Perhaps."

He was too powerful for the room; he didn't go with the cretonne. Did his sister sit here, while they, in another room—or did they send her out on errands while they made love?

Well, I had seen the man; there wasn't anything to stay for—except all the other questions that now were released by the sight of him: Where had they met? Had she made the first move? What had she seen in him? How long, how often had they been lovers? There were words she had written that I knew by heart: "I have no need to write to you or talk to you. . . . I know I am only beginning to love, but already I want to abandon everything, everybody but you." And I stared up at the strawberry mark on his cheek and thought, there is no safety anywhere; a humpback, a cripple—they all have the trigger that sets love off.

"What was the real purpose of your coming?" He suddenly broke into my thoughts.

"I told Miss Smythe. A man called Wilson—"

"I don't remember your face, but I remember your son's." He made a short frustrated gesture as though he wanted to touch the boy's hand; his eyes had a kind of abstract tenderness. He said, "You don't have to be afraid of me. I am used to people coming here. I assure you, I only want to be of use."

Miss Smythe explained. "People are often so shy." I couldn't for the life of me think what it was all about.

"I was just looking for a man called Wilcox."

"You know that *I* know there's no such man."

"If you would lend me a telephone directory I could check his address—"

"Sit down again," he said and brooded gloomily over the boy.

"I must be going. Arthur's feeling better, and Wilcox—" His ambiguity made me ill at ease.

"You can go if you want to, of course, but can't you leave the boy here, if only for half an hour? I want to talk to him." It occurred to me that he had recognized Parkis's assistant and was going to cross-question him. I said, "Anything you want to ask him you can ask me." Every time he turned his unmarked cheek towards me my anger grew; every time I saw that raw strawberry flush it died away, and I couldn't believe—any more than I could believe that lust existed here among the flowered cretonnes, with Miss Smythe getting tea. But despair can always produce an answer, and despair asked me now, "Would you so much rather it was love and not lust?"

"You and I are too old," he said. "But the schoolmasters and the priests—they've only just begun to corrupt him with their lies."

"I don't know what the hell you mean," I said, and added quickly, "I'm sorry," to Miss Smythe.

"There you are, you see," he said. "Hell, and if I angered you, as like as not you'd say, 'My God.'"

It seemed to me that I had shocked him. He might be a non-conformist minister; Miss Smythe had said he worked on Sundays; but how horribly bizarre that a man like that should be Sarah's lover. Suddenly it diminished her importance; her love affair became a joke; she herself might be used as a comic anecdote at my next dinner party. For a moment I was free of her.

The boy said, "I feel sick. Can I have some more orangeade?"

Miss Smythe said, "My dear, I think you'd better not."

"Really, I must be taking him away. It's been very good of you." I tried to keep the strawberry mark well in view. I said, "I'm very sorry if I offended you at all. It was quite by accident. I don't happen to share your religious beliefs."

He looked at me with surprise. "But I have none. I believe in nothing."

"I thought you objected—"

"I hate the trappings that are left over. Forgive me. I go too far, Mr. Bridges, I know, but I'm sometimes afraid that people will be reminded even by conventional words —good-bye, for instance. If only I could believe that my grandson would not even know what a word like 'god' had meant to us any more than a word in Swahili."

"Have you a grandson?"

He said gloomily, "I have no children. I envy you your boy. It's a great duty and a great responsibility."

"What did you want to ask him?"

"I wanted him to feel at home here, because then he might return. There are so many things one wants to tell a child—how the world came into existence. I wanted to tell him about death. I wanted to rid him of all the lies they inject at school."

"Rather a lot to do in half an hour."

"One can sow a seed."

I said maliciously, "That comes out of the Gospels."

"Oh, I've been corrupted too. You don't need to tell me that."

"Do people really come to you—on the quiet?"

"You'd be surprised," Miss Smythe said. "People are longing for a message of hope."

"Hope?"

"Yes, hope," Smythe said. "Can't you see what hope there'd be if everybody in the world knew that there was nothing else but what we have here—no future compensation, rewards, punishments?" His face had a crazy nobility when the strawberry mark was hidden. "Then we'd begin to make this world like heaven."

"There's a terrible lot to be explained first," I said.

"Can I show you my library?"

"It's the best rationalist library in South London," Miss Smythe explained.

"I don't need to be converted, Mr. Smythe. I believe in nothing, as it is. Except now and then."

"It's the now and thens we have to deal with."

"The odd thing is that those are the moments of hope."

"Pride can masquerade as hope. Or selfishness."

"I don't think that has anything to do with it at all. It happens suddenly, for no reason, a scent—"

"Ah," Smythe said, "the construction of a flower, the argument from design, all that business about a watch requiring a watchmaker. It's old-fashioned. Schwenigen answered all that twenty-five years ago. Let me show you—"

"Not today. I must really take the boy home."

Again he made that gesture of frustrated tenderness, like a lover who has been rejected. I wondered suddenly from how many deathbeds he had been excluded. I found that I wanted to give him some message of hope too, but then the cheek turned and I saw only the arrogant actor's face. I preferred him when he was pitiable, inadequate, out of date. Ayer, Russell—they were the fashion today, but I doubted whether there were many logical positivists in his library. He had only the crusaders, not the detached.

At the door—I noticed that he didn't use that dangerous term good-bye—I shot directly at his handsome cheek. "You should meet a friend of mine, Mrs. Miles. She's interested—" and then I stopped. The shot had gone home. The strawberry mark seemed to spread all across his face, and I heard Miss Smythe say, "Oh, my dear," as he turned abruptly away. There was no doubt that I had given him pain, but the pain was mine as well as his. I wished my shot had gone astray.

In the gutter outside, Parkis's boy was sick. I let him vomit, standing there, wondering, has he lost her too? Is there no end to this? Have I now got to discover Y?

VIII

Parkis said, "It was really very easy, sir. There was such a crush, and Mrs. Miles thought I was one of his friends from the Ministry, and Mr. Miles thought I was one of *her* friends."

"Was it a good cocktail party?" I asked, remembering again that first meeting and the sight of Sarah with the stranger.

"Highly successful, I should say, sir, but Mrs. Miles seemed a bit out of sorts. A very nasty cough, she's got." I heard him with pleasure; perhaps at this party there had been no alcove kissing or touching. He laid a brown paper parcel on my desk and said with pride, "I knew the way to her room from the maid. If anyone had taken notice of me, I should have been looking for the toilet, but nobody did. There it was, out on her desk; she must have worked on it that day. Of course she may be very cautious, but my experience of diaries is they always give things away. People invent their little codes, but you soon see through them, sir. Or they leave out things, but you soon learn what they leave out." While he spoke I unwrapped the book and opened it. "It's human nature, sir, that if you keep a diary you want to remember things. Why keep it, otherwise?"

"Did you look at this?" I asked.

"I ascertained its nature, sir, and from one entry judged she wasn't of the cautious type."

"It's not this year's," I said. "It's two years old."

For a moment he was dashed.

"It will serve my purpose," I said.

"It would do the trick as well, sir—if nothing's been condoned."

The journal was written in a big account book, the familiar bold handwriting crossed by the red and blue lines. There were not daily entries, and I was able to reassure Parkis. "It covers several years."

"I suppose something must have made her take it out to read." Is it possible, I wondered, that some memory of me, of our affair, had crossed her mind this very day, that something may have troubled her peace?

I said to Parkis, "I'm glad to have this, very glad. You know, I really think we can close our account now."

"I hope you feel satisfied, sir."

"Quite satisfied."

"And that you'll so write to Mr. Savage, sir. He gets the bad reports from clients, but the good ones never get written. The more a client's satisfied, the more he wants to forget, to put us right out of mind. You can hardly blame them."

"I'll write."

"And thank you, sir, for being kind to the boy. He was a bit upset, but I know how it is—it's difficult to draw the line over ices with a boy like Lance. He gets them out of you with hardly a word said." I longed to read, but Parkis lingered. Perhaps he didn't really trust me to remember him and wanted to impress more firmly on my memory those hangdog eyes, that penurious moustache. "I've enjoyed our association, sir—if one can talk of enjoying under the sad circumstances. We don't always work for real gentlemen, even when they have titles. I had a peer of the realm once, sir, who flew into a rage when I gave him my report, as though I were the guilty party myself. It's a discouraging thing, sir. The more you succeed the more glad they are to see the last of you."

I was very conscious of wanting to see the last of Parkis, and his words woke my sense of guilt. I couldn't hurry the man away. He said, "I've been thinking, sir, I'd like to give you a little memento—but then that's just what you wouldn't want to receive."

How strange it is to be liked. It automatically awakens a certain loyalty. So I lied to Parkis. "I've always enjoyed our talks."

"Which started, sir, so inauspiciously. With that silly mistake."

"Did you ever tell your boy?"

"Yes, sir, but only after some days, after the success with the waste-paper basket. That took away the sting."

I looked down at the book and read: "So happy. M. returns tomorrow." I wondered for a moment who M. was. How strange and unfamiliar to think that one had been loved, that one's presence had once had the power to make a difference between happiness and dullness in another's day.

"But if you really wouldn't resent a memento, sir—"

"Of course I wouldn't, Parkis."

"I have something here, sir, that might be of interest and use." He took out of his pocket an object wrapped in tissue paper and slid it shyly across the desk towards me. I unwrapped it. It was a cheap ash tray, marked "Hotel Metropole, Brightlingsea." "There's quite a history, sir, with that. You remember the Bolton case."

"I can't say I do."

"It made a great stir, sir, at the time. Lady Bolton, her maid, and the man, sir. All discovered together. That ash tray stood beside the bed. On the lady's side."

"You must have collected quite a little museum."

"I should have given it to Mr. Savage—he took a particular interest—but I'm glad now, sir, I didn't. I think you'll find the inscription will evoke comment when your friends put out their cigarettes, and there's your answer pat—the Bolton case. They'll all want to hear more of that."

"It sounds sensational."

"It's all human nature, sir, isn't it, and human love. Though I *was* surprised. Not having expected the third. And the room not large or fashionable. Mrs. Parkis was alive then, but I didn't like to tell her the details. She got disturbed by things."

"I'll certainly treasure the memento," I said.

"If ash trays could speak, sir."

"Indeed, yes."

But even Parkis, with that profound thought, had finished up his words. A last pressure of the hand, a little sticky—perhaps it had been in contact with Lance's—and he was gone. He was not one of those whom one expects to see again.

Then I opened Sarah's journal. I thought first I would look for that day in June 1944 when everything ended, and, after I had discovered the reason for that, there were other dates from which I could learn exactly, checking them with my diary, how it was that her love had petered out. I wanted to treat this as a document in a case—one of

Parkis's cases—should be treated, but I hadn't that degree of calmness, for what I found when I opened the journal was not what I was expecting. Hate and suspicion and envy had driven me so far away that I read her words like a declaration of love from a stranger. I had expected plenty of evidence against her—hadn't I so often caught her out in lies?—and now, here in writing that I could believe as I couldn't believe her voice, was the complete answer. For it was the last couple of pages I read first, and I read them again at the end to make sure. It's a strange thing to discover and to believe that you are loved, when you know that nothing is there for anybody but a parent or a God to love.

BOOK THREE

I

. . . anything left when we'd finished but You. For either of us. I might have taken a lifetime spending a little love at a time, doling it out here and there, on this man and that. But even the first time, in the hotel near Paddington, we spent all we had. You were there, teaching us to squander, like You taught the rich man, so that one day we might have nothing left except this love of You. But You are too good to me. When I ask You for pain, You give me peace. Give it him too. Give him my peace—he needs it more.

February 12, 1946.

Two days ago I had such a sense of peace and quiet and love. Life was going to be happy again, but last night I dreamed I was walking up a long staircase to meet Maurice at the top. I was still happy because when I reached the top of the staircase we were going to make love. I called to him that I was coming, but it wasn't Maurice's voice that answered; it was a stranger's that boomed like a foghorn warning lost ships, and scared me. I thought, he's let his flat and gone away and I don't know where he is, and going down the stairs again the water rose beyond my waist and the hall was thick with mist. Then I woke up. I'm not at peace any more. I just want him like I used to in the old days. I want to be eating sandwiches with him. I want to be drinking with him in a bar. I'm tired and I don't want any more pain. I want Maurice. I want ordinary corrupt human love. Dear God, You know I want to want Your pain, but I don't want it now. Please take it away for a while and give it me another time.

After that I started the book from the beginning. She hadn't entered the journal every day, and I had no wish to read every entry. The theatres she had been to with Henry, the restaurants, the parties—all that life of which I knew nothing had the power to hurt.

June 12, 1944.

Sometimes I get so tired of trying to convince him that I love him and shall love him forever. He pounces on my words like a barrister and twists them. I know he is afraid of that desert which would be round him if our love were to end, but he can't realize that I feel exactly the same. What he says aloud, I say to myself silently and write it here. What can one build in the desert? Sometimes after a day when we have made love many times, I wonder whether it isn't possible to come to an end of sex, and I know that he is wondering too and is afraid of that point where the desert begins. What do we do in the desert if we lose each other? How does one go on living after that?

He is jealous of the past and the present and the future. His love is like a medieval chastity belt: only when he is there, with me, in me, does he feel safe. If only I could make him feel secure, then we could love peacefully, happily, not savagely, inordinately, and the desert would recede out of sight. For a lifetime perhaps.

If one could believe in God, would he fill the desert?

I have always wanted to be liked or admired. I feel a terrible insecurity if a man turns on me, if I lose a friend. I don't even want to lose a husband. I want everything, all the time, everywhere. I'm afraid of the desert. God loves you, they say in the churches; God is everything. People who believe that don't need admiration, they don't need to sleep with a man, they feel safe. But I can't invent a belief.

All today Maurice has been sweet to me. He tells me often that he has never loved another woman so much. He thinks that by saying it often he will make me believe it. But I believe it simply because I love him in exactly the same way. If I stopped loving him, I would cease to believe in his love. If I loved God, then I would believe in his love for me. It's not enough to need it. We have to love first, and I don't know how. But I need it, how I need it.

All day he was sweet. Only once, when a man's name was mentioned, I saw his eyes move away. He thinks I still sleep with other men, and if I did, would it matter so much? If sometimes he has a woman, do I complain? I wouldn't rob him of some small companionship in the desert if we can't have each other there. Sometimes I think that if the time came he would refuse me even a glass of water; he would drive me into such complete isolation that I would be alone with nothing and nobody —like a hermit, but they were never alone, or so they say. I am so muddled. What are we doing to each other? Because I know that I am doing to him exactly what he is doing to me. We are sometimes so happy, and never in our lives have we known more unhappiness. It's as if we were working together on the same statue, cutting it out of each other's misery. But I don't even know the design.

June 17, 1944.

Yesterday I went home with him, and we did the usual things. I haven't the nerve to put them down, but I'd like to, because now when I'm writing it's already tomorrow and I'm afraid of getting to the end of yesterday. As long as I go on writing, yesterday is today and we are still together.

While I waited for him yesterday there were speakers out on the Common: the I.L.P. and the Communist party, and the man who just tells jokes, and there was a man attacking Christianity—the Rationalist Society of South London or some name like that. He would have been good-looking if it hadn't been for the strawberry mark on one cheek. There were very few people in his audience and no hecklers. He was attacking something dead already, and I wondered why he took the trouble. I stayed and listened for a few minutes; he was arguing against the arguments for a God. I hadn't really known there were any—except this cowardly need I feel of not being alone.

I had a sudden fear that Henry might have changed his mind and sent a telegram to say that he would be home. I never know what I fear most—my disappointment or Maurice's disappointment. It works the same way with both of us: we pick quarrels. I am angry with myself, and he is angry with me. I went home, and there was no telegram, and I was ten minutes late in meeting Maurice and began to be angry so as to meet his anger, and then unexpectedly he was sweet to me.

We had never before had quite so long a day, and there was all the night to follow. We bought lettuce and rolls and the butter ration—we didn't want much to eat, and it was very warm. It's warm now too; everybody will say, "What a lovely summer," and I'm in a train going into the country to join Henry, and everything's over forever. I'm scared; this is the desert, and there's nobody, nothing, for miles and miles around. If I were in London I might be killed quickly, but if I were in London I'd go to the telephone and ring the only number I know by heart. I often forget my own; I suppose Freud would say that I want to forget it because it's Henry's number too. But I love Henry; I want him to be happy. I only hate him today because he *is* happy, and I am not and Maurice is not, and he won't know a thing. He'll say I look tired and think it's the curse—he no longer bothers to keep the count of those days.

This evening the sirens went—I mean last evening of course, but what does it matter? In the desert there's no time. But I can come out of the desert when I want to. I can catch a train home tomorrow and ring him up on the telephone. Henry will be still in the country perhaps, and we can spend the night together. A vow's not all that important—a vow to somebody I've never known, to somebody I don't really believe in. Nobody will know that I've broken a vow, except me and him—and he doesn't exist, does he? He can't exist. You can't have a merciful God and this despair.

If I went back, where would we be? Where we were yesterday before the sirens went, and the year before that. Angry with each other for fear of the end, wondering what we should do with life when there was nothing left. I needn't wonder any more; there's nothing to fear any more. This is the end. But, dear God, what shall I do with this desire to love?

Why do I write "dear God"? He isn't dear—not to me

he isn't. If he exists, then he put the thought of this vow into my mind, and I hate him for it. I hate. Every few minutes a grey stone church and a public house run backwards down the line; the desert is full of churches and public houses—and multiple stores, and men on bicycles, and grass and cows, and factory chimneys. You see them through the sand like fish through the water in a tank. And Henry waits too in the tank, raising his muzzle for my kiss.

We paid no attention to the sirens. They didn't matter. We weren't afraid of dying that way. But then the raid went on and on. It wasn't an ordinary raid; the papers aren't allowed to say yet, but everybody knows. This was the new thing we had been warned about. Maurice went downstairs to see if there was anyone in the basement— he was afraid about me, and I was afraid about him. I knew something was going to happen.

He hadn't been gone two minutes when there was an explosion in the street. His room was at the back, and nothing happened except that the door was sucked open and some plaster fell, but I knew that he was at the front of the house when the bomb fell. I went down the stairs; they were cluttered with rubbish and broken banisters, and the hall was in an awful mess. I didn't see Maurice at first, and then I saw his arm coming out from under the door. I touched his hand; I could have sworn it was a dead hand. When two people have loved each other, they can't disguise a lack of tenderness in a kiss, and wouldn't I have recognized life if there was any of it left, in touching his hand? I knew that if I took his hand and pulled it towards me it would come away, all by itself, from under the door. Now, of course, I know that this was hysteria. I was cheated. He wasn't dead. Is one responsible for what one promises in hysteria? Or what promises one breaks? I'm hysterical now, writing all this down. But there's not a single person anywhere to whom I can even say I'm unhappy because they would ask me why, and the questions would begin and I would break down. I mustn't break down because I must protect Henry. Oh, to hell with Henry, to hell with Henry. I want somebody who'll accept the truth about me and doesn't need protection. If I'm a bitch and a fake, is there nobody who will love a bitch and a fake?

I knelt down on the floor; I was mad to do such a thing; I never even had to do it as a child—my parents never believed in prayer, any more than I do. I hadn't any idea what to say. Maurice was dead. Extinct. There wasn't such a thing as a soul. Even the half-happiness I gave him was drained out of him like blood. He would never have the chance to be happy again—with anybody, I thought; somebody else could have loved him and made him happier than I could, but now he won't have that chance. I knelt and put my head on the bed and wished I could believe. Dear God, I said—why dear, why dear?—make me believe. I can't believe. Make me. I said, I'm a bitch and a fake and I hate myself. I can't do anything of myself. *Make* me believe. I shut my eyes tight, and I pressed my nails into the palms of my hands until I could feel nothing but the pain, and I said, I will believe. Let him be alive, and I *will* believe. Give him a chance. Let him have his happiness. Do this, and I'll believe. But that wasn't enough. It doesn't hurt to believe.

So I said, I love him and I'll do anything if You'll make him alive. I said very slowly, I'll give him up forever, only let him be alive with a chance, and I pressed and pressed and I could feel the skin break, and I said, people can love without seeing each other, can't they, they love You all their lives without seeing You, and then he came in at the door, and he was alive, and I thought now the agony of being without him starts, and I wished he was safely back dead again under the door.

July 9, 1944.

Caught the 8:30 with Henry. Empty first-class carriage. Henry read aloud the Proceedings of the Royal Commission. Caught taxi at Paddington and dropped Henry at the Ministry. Made him promise to be home tonight. Taxi man made mistake and drove me to the south side, past Number 14. Door mended and front windows boarded. It is horrible feeling dead. One wants to feel alive again in any way. When I got to the north side there were old letters that hadn't been forwarded because I'd told them, "Forward nothing." Old book catalogues, old bills, a letter marked "Urgent. Please forward." I wanted to open it and see if I was alive still, but I tore it up with the catalogues.

July 10, 1944.

I thought, I shall not be breaking my promise if accidentally on the Common I run into Maurice, and so I went out after breakfast and again after lunch and again in the early evening, walking about and never seeing him. I couldn't stay out after six because Henry had guests for dinner. The speakers were there again as they were in June, and the man with the strawberry mark was still attacking Christianity and nobody was caring. I thought, if only he could convince me that you don't have to keep a promise to someone you don't believe in, that miracles don't happen, and I went and listened to him for a while, but all the time I was looking round in case Maurice might come in sight. He talked about the date of the Gospels and how the earliest one wasn't written within a hundred years of Christ being born. I had never realized they were as early as that, but I couldn't see that it mattered much when the legend began. And then he told us that Christ never claimed to be God in the Gospels—but was there such a man as Christ at all, and what do the Gospels matter anyway, compared with this pain of waiting around and not seeing Maurice? A woman with grey hair distributed little cards on which his name was printed, Richard Smythe, and his address in Cedar Road, and there was an invitation to anybody to come and talk to him in private. Some people refused to take the cards and walked away as though the woman was asking for a subscription, and others dropped them on

the grass (I saw her pick some up, for economy's sake
I suppose). It seemed very sad—the strawberry mark,
and talking about something nobody was interested in,
and the cards dropped were like offers of friendship
turned down. I put the card in my pocket and hoped he
saw me do it.

Sir William Mallock came to dinner. He was one of
Lloyd George's advisers on National Insurance, very old
and important. Henry of course has nothing to do with
pensions any longer, but he keeps an interest in the subject and likes to recall those days. Wasn't it widows' pensions he was working on when Maurice and I had dinner
for the first time and everything started? Henry began a
long argument with Mallock, full of statistics about
whether if widows' pensions were raised another shilling
they would reach the same height as ten years ago. They
disagreed about the cost of living, and it was a very
academic argument because they both said the country
couldn't afford to raise them anyway. I had to talk to
Henry's chief in the Ministry of Home Security, and I
couldn't think of anything to talk about but the V-1s,
and I longed suddenly to tell everybody about coming
downstairs and finding Maurice buried. I wanted to say,
I was naked, of course, because I hadn't had time to
dress. Would Sir William Mallock have even turned his
head, or would Henry have heard? He has a wonderful
knack of hearing nothing but the subject in hand, and
the subject in hand at that moment was the cost-of-living
index for 1943. I was naked, I wanted to say, because
Maurice and I had been making love all the evening.

I looked at Henry's chief. He was a man called Dunstan. He had a broken nose, and his battered face looked like a potter's error—a rejected-for-export face. All he would do, I thought, was smile; he wouldn't be cross or indifferent; he would accept it as something that human beings did. I had a sense that I had only to make a move and he would reply to it. I wondered, why shouldn't I? Why shouldn't I escape from this desert if only for half an hour? I haven't promised anything about strangers, only about Maurice. I can't be alone for the rest of my life with Henry, nobody admiring me, nobody excited by me, listening to Henry talking to other people, fossilizing under the drip of conversation like that bowler hat in the Cheddar Caves.

July 15, 1944.

Had lunch with Dunstan at the Jardin des Gourmets. He said . . .

July 21, 1944.

Had drinks with Dunstan at home, while he waited for Henry. All went on to . . .

July 22, 1944.

Had dinner with D. He came home afterwards for another drink. But it didn't work, it didn't work.

July 23–July 30, 1944.

D. telephoned. Said I was out. Started on tour with Henry. Civil Defence in Southern England. Conferences with Chief Wardens and Borough Engineers. Blast problems. Deep shelter problems. The problem of pretending to be alive. Henry and I sleeping side by side night after night like figures on tombs. In the new reinforced shelter at Bigwell-on-Sea the Chief Warden kissed me. Henry had gone ahead into the second chamber with the mayor and the engineer, and I stopped the Warden, touching his arm and asking him a question about the steel bunks, something stupid about why there weren't double bunks for the married. I meant him to want to kiss me. He twisted me round against a bunk, so that the metal made a line of pain across my back, and kissed me. Then he looked so astonished that I laughed and kissed him back. But nothing worked. Will it never work again? The mayor came back with Henry. He was saying, "At a pinch we can find room for two hundred."

That night, when Henry was at an official dinner, I asked Trunks to get me Maurice's number. I lay on my bed, waiting for it to come through. I said to God, I've kept my promise for six weeks. I can't believe in you, I can't love you, but I've kept my promise. If I don't come alive again, I'm going to be a slut, just a slut. I'm going to destroy myself quite deliberately. Every year I'll be more used. Will you like that any better than if I break my promise? I'll be like those women in bars who laugh too much and have three men with them, touching them without intimacy. I'm falling in pieces already.

I kept the receiver tucked in my shoulder, and the exchange said, "We are ringing your number now." I said to God, if he answers, I'll go back tomorrow. I knew exactly where the telephone stood beside his bed. Once I had knocked it down in my sleep, hitting out with my fist. A girl's voice said, "Hello," and I nearly rang off. I had wanted Maurice to be happy, but had I wanted him to find happiness quite so quickly? I felt a bit sick in the stomach until logic came to my aid, and I made my brain argue with me—why shouldn't he? You left him; you want him to be happy.

I said, "Could I speak to Mr. Bendrix?" But everything had gone flat. Perhaps he wouldn't even want me to break my promise now; perhaps he had found somebody who would stay with him, have meals with him, go with him to places, sleep with him night after night till it was sweet and customary, answer his telephone for him.

Then the voice said, "Mr. Bendrix isn't here. He's gone away for a few weeks. I've borrowed the flat."

I rang off. At first I was happy, and then I was miserable again. I didn't know where he was. We were not in touch—in the same desert, seeking the same water-holes perhaps, but out of sight, always alone. For it wouldn't be a desert if we were together. I said to God, so that's it. I begin to believe in you, and if I believe in you I shall hate you. I have free will to break my promise, haven't I? But I haven't the power to gain anything from breaking it. You let me telephone, but then you close the door in my face. You let me sin, but you take away the fruits of my sin. You let me try to escape with D., but you don't allow me to enjoy it. You make me drive love out, and then you say, "There's no lust left for you either." What do you expect me to do now, God? Where do I go from here?

When I was at school I learned about a king—one of the Henrys, the one who had Becket murdered—and he swore, when he saw his birthplace burned by his enemies, that because God had done that to him—"because You have robbed me of the town I love most, the place where I was born and bred, I will rob You of that which You love most in me." Odd how I've remembered that prayer after sixteen years. A king swore it on his horse seven hundred years ago, and I pray it now, in a hotel room at Bigwell-on-Sea—Bigwell Regis. I'm going to rob you, God, of what you love most in me. I've never known the Lord's Prayer by heart, but I remember that one—is it a prayer? Of what you love most in me.

What do you love most? If I believed in you, I suppose I'd believe in the immortal soul, but is that what you love? Can you really see it there under the skin? Even a God can't love something that doesn't exist, he can't love something he cannot see. When he looks at me, does he see something I can't see? It must be lovely if he is able to love it. That's asking me to believe too much, that there's anything lovely in me. I want men to admire me, but that's a trick you learn at school—a movement of the eyes, a tone of voice, a touch of the hand on the shoulder or the head. If they think you admire them, they will admire you because of your good taste, and when they admire you, you have an illusion for a moment that there's something to admire. All my life I've tried to live in that illusion—a soothing drug that allows me to forget that I'm a bitch and a fake. But what are you supposed to love, then, in the bitch and the fake? Where do you find that immortal soul they talk about? Where do you see this lovely thing in me—in me, of all people? I can understand you can find it in Henry—my

Henry, I mean. He's gentle and good and patient. You can find it in Maurice, who thinks he hates, and loves, loves all the time—even his enemies. But in this bitch and fake where do you find anything to love?

Tell me that, God, and I'll set about robbing you of it forever.

How did the king keep his promise? I wish I could remember. I can remember nothing more about him than that he let the monks scourge him over the tomb of Becket. That doesn't sound like the answer. It must have happened before.

Henry's away again tonight. If I go down into the bar and pick a man up and take him onto the beach and lie with him among the sand dunes, won't I be robbing you of what you love most? But it doesn't work. It doesn't work any longer. I can't hurt you if I don't get any pleasure from it. I might as well stick pins in myself like those people in the desert. The desert. I want to do something that I enjoy and that will hurt you. Otherwise what is it but mortification, and that's like an expression of belief? And believe me, God, I don't believe in you yet, I don't believe in you yet.

IV

September 12, 1944.

Lunched at Peter Jones and bought new lamp for Henry's study. A prim lunch surrounded by other women. Not a man anywhere. It was like being part of a regiment. Almost a sense of peace. Afterwards went to a news cinema in Piccadilly and saw ruins in Normandy and the arrival of an American politician. Nothing to do till seven when Henry would be back. Had a couple of drinks by myself. It was a mistake. Have I got to give up drinking too? If I eliminate everything, how will I exist? I was somebody who loved Maurice and went with men and enjoyed my drinks. What happens if you drop all the things that make you I? Henry came in. I could tell he was very pleased about something; he obviously wanted me to ask him what it was, but I wouldn't. So in the end he had to tell me. "They are recommending me for an O.B.E."

"What's that?" I asked.

He was rather dashed that I didn't know. He explained that the next stage, in a year or two, when he was head of his department, would be a C.B.E. "And after that," he said, "when I retire they'll probably give me a K.B.E."

"It's awfully confusing," I said. "Couldn't you stick to the same letters?"

"Wouldn't you like to be Lady Miles?" Henry said, and I thought angrily, all I want in the world is to be Mrs. Bendrix, and I have given up that hope forever. Lady Miles, who doesn't have a lover and doesn't drink but talks to Sir William Mallock about pensions. Where would *I* be all that time?

Last night I looked at Henry when he was asleep. So long as I was what the law considers the guilty party I could watch him with affection, as though he were a child who needed my protection. Now I was what they called innocent, I was maddened continually by him. He had a secretary who sometimes rang him up at home. She would say, "Oh, Mrs. Miles, is H.M. in?" All the secretaries used those unbearable initials, not intimate but companionable. H.M., I thought, looking at him asleep. H.M. His Majesty and His Majesty's consort. Sometimes in his sleep he smiled, a moderate brief civil-servant smile, as much as to say, yes, very amusing, but now we'd better get on with the job, hadn't we?

I said to him once, "Have you ever had an affair with a secretary?"

"Affair?"

"Love affair."

"No, of course not. What makes you think such a thing?"

"I don't know. I just wondered."

"I've never loved any other woman," he said and began to read the evening paper. I couldn't help wondering, is my husband so unattractive that no woman has ever wanted him? Except me, of course. I must have wanted him, in a way, once, but I've forgotten why, and I was too young to know what I was choosing. It's so unfair. While I loved Maurice, I loved Henry, and now I'm what they call good, I don't love anyone at all. And you least of all.

V

May 8, 1945.

Went down to St. James's Park in the evening to watch them celebrate V-E Day. It was very quiet beside the floodlit water between the Horse Guards and the palace. Nobody shouted or sang or got drunk. People sat on the grass in twos, holding hands. I suppose they were happy because this was peace and there were no more bombs. I said to Henry, "I don't like the peace."

"I'm wondering where I shall be drafted from the Ministry of Home Security."

"Ministry of Information?" I asked, trying to be interested.

"No, no, I wouldn't take it. It's full of temporary civil servants. How would you like the Home Office?"

"Anything, Henry, that pleased you," I said. Then the Royal Family came out on the balcony, and the crowd sang very decorously. They weren't leaders like Hitler, Stalin, Churchill, Roosevelt; they were just a family who hadn't done any harm to anybody. I wanted Maurice beside me. I wanted to begin again. I wanted to be one of a family too.

"Very moving, isn't it?" Henry said. "Well, we can all sleep quiet at night now," as though we ever did anything else at night but just sleep quiet.

September 16, 1945.

I have got to be sensible. Two days ago when I was clearing out my old bag—Henry suddenly gave me a new one as a "peace present"; it must have cost him a lot of money—I found a card saying "Richard Smythe 16 Cedar Road 4-6 daily for private advice. Anyone welcome." I thought, I have been pulled about long enough. Now I'll take a different medicine. If he can persuade me that nothing happened, that my promise doesn't count, I'll write to Maurice and ask him if he wants to go on again. Perhaps I'll even leave Henry. I don't know. But first I've got to be sensible. I won't be hysterical any more. I'll be reasonable. So I went and rang the bell in Cedar Road.

Now I'm trying to remember what happened. Miss Smythe made tea, and after tea she went and left me alone with her brother. He asked me what my difficulties were. I sat on a chintz sofa, and he sat on a rather hard chair with a cat on his lap. He stroked the cat and he had rather beautiful hands, and I didn't like them. I almost liked the strawberry mark better, but he chose to sit showing me only his good cheek.

I said, "Will you tell me why you are so certain there isn't a God?"

He watched his own hands stroking the cat, and I felt sorry for him because he was proud of his hands. If his face hadn't been marked, perhaps he would have had no pride.

"You've listened to me speaking on the Common?"

"Yes," I said.

"I have to put things very simply there To sting people into thinking for themselves. You've started thinking for yourself?"

"I suppose so."

"What church have you been brought up in?"

"None."

"So you aren't a Christian?"

"I may have been christened—it's a social convention, isn't it?"

"If you haven't any faith, why do you want my help?"

Why indeed? I couldn't tell him about Maurice under the door, and my promise. Not yet I couldn't. And that wasn't the whole point, for how many promises I've made and broken in a lifetime. Why did this promise stay, like an ugly vase a friend has given, and one waits for a maid to break it, and year after year she breaks the things one values and the ugly vase remains? I had never really faced his question, and now he had to repeat it.

I said, "I'm not sure that I don't believe. But I don't want to."

"Tell me," he said, and because he forgot the beauty of his own hands and turned towards me his ugly stained cheek, forgetting himself in the desire to help, I found myself talking—about that night and the bomb falling and the stupid vow.

"And you really believe," he said, "that perhaps—"

"Yes."

"Think of the thousands of people all over the world, praying now, and their prayers aren't answered."

"There were thousands of people dying in Palestine when Lazarus—"

"We don't believe that story, do we, you and I?" he said with a kind of complicity.

"Of course not, but millions of people have. They must have thought it reasonable."

"People don't demand that a thing be reasonable if their emotions are touched. Lovers aren't reasonable, are they?"

"Can you explain away love too?" I asked.

"Oh, yes," he said. "The desire to possess in some, like avarice; in others the desire to surrender, to lose the sense of responsibility, the wish to be admired. Sometimes just the wish to be able to talk, to unburden yourself to someone who won't be bored. The desire to find again a father or a mother. And of course under it all the biological motive."

I thought, it's all true, but isn't there something over? I've dug up all that in myself, in Maurice too, but still the spade hasn't touched rock. "And the love of God?" I asked him.

"It's all the same. Man made God in his own image, so it's natural he should love him. You know those distorting mirrors at fairs. Man's made a beautifying mirror too, in which he sees himself lovely and powerful and just and wise. It's his idea of himself. He recognizes himself easier than in the distorting mirror, which only makes him laugh, but how he loves himself in the other!"

When he spoke of distorting and beautifying mirrors I couldn't remember what we were talking about for the thought of all those times since adolescence when he had looked in mirrors and tried to make them beautifying and not distorting simply by the way he held his head. I wondered why he hadn't grown a beard long enough to hide the stain; won't the hair grow, or was it because he hated deception? I had an idea that he was a man who really loved the truth, but there was that word "love"

again, and it was only too obvious into how many desires his love of truth could be split: a compensation for
the injury of his birth, the desire for power, the wish to
be admired all the more because the poor haunted face
would never cause physical desire. I had an enormous
wish to touch it with my hand, to comfort it with words
of love as permanent as the wound. It was like when I
saw Maurice under the door. I wanted to pray, to offer
up some inordinate sacrifice if only he could be healed;
but now there was no sacrifice left for me to offer.

"My dear," he said, "leave the idea of God out of this.
It's just a question of your lover and your husband. Don't
confuse the thing with phantoms."

"But how do I decide, if there's no such thing as love?"

"You have to decide what will be the happiest in the
long run."

"Do you believe in happiness?"

"I don't believe in any absolute."

I thought, the only happiness he ever gets is this: the
idea that he can comfort, advise, help; the idea that he
can be of use. It drives him every week onto the Common, to talk to people who move away, never asking
questions, dropping his cards on the turf. How often does
anybody really come as I have come today? I asked him,
"Do you have many callers?"

"No," he said. His love of truth was greater than his
pride. He said, "You are the first—for a very long time."

"It's been good to talk to you," I said. "You've cleared
my mind quite a lot." It was the only comfort one could
give him—to feed his illusion.

He said shyly, "If you could spare the time, we could

really start at the beginning and go to the root of things—I mean the philosophical arguments and the historical evidence."

I suppose I must have made some evasive reply, for he went on, "It's really important. We mustn't despise our enemies. They have a case."

"They have?"

"It's not a sound one, except superficially. It's specious."

He watched me with anxiety. I think he was wondering whether I was one of those who walked away. It seemed a little thing to ask when he said nervously, "An hour a week. It would help you a great deal." And I thought, haven't I all of time now? I can read a book or go to a cinema, and I don't read the words or remember the pictures. Myself and my own misery drum in my ears and fill my eyes. For a minute this afternoon I forgot them. "Yes," I said, "I'll come. It's good of you to spare the time," I said, shovelling all the hope I could into his lap, praying to the God he was promising to cure me of, Let me be of use to him.

October 2, 1945.

It was very hot today and it dripped with rain. So I went into the dark church at the corner of Park Road to sit down for a while. Henry was at home, and I didn't want to see him. I try to remember to be kind at breakfast, kind at lunch when he's home, kind at dinner; and sometimes I forget, and he's kind back. Two people being kind to each other for a lifetime. When I came in and sat down and looked round I realized it was a Roman church, full of plaster statues and bad art, realistic art. I hated the statues, the crucifix, all the emphasis on the human body. I was trying to escape from the human body and all it needed. I thought I could believe in some kind of a God that bore no relation to ourselves, something vague, amorphous, cosmic, to which I had promised something and which had given me something in return —a Thing which had stretched out of the vague into the concrete human life, like a powerful vapour moving among the chairs and walls. One day I too would become part of that vapour; I would escape myself forever. And then I came into that dark church in Park Road and saw the bodies standing around me on all the altars—the hideous plaster statues with their complacent faces—and I remembered that they believed in the resurrection of the body, the body I wanted destroyed forever. I had done so much injury with this body. How could I want to preserve any of it for eternity? And suddenly I remembered a phrase of Richard's, about human beings inventing doctrines to satisfy their desires, and I thought, how wrong he is. If I were to invent a doctrine it would be that the body was never born again, that it rotted with last year's vermin. It's strange how the human mind swings back and forth, from one extreme to another. Does truth lie at some point of the pendulum's swing, at a point where it never rests—not in the dull perpendicular mean, where it dangles in the end like a windless flag, but at an angle, nearer one extreme than another? If only a miracle could stop the pendulum at an angle of sixty degrees, one would believe the truth was there. Well, the pendulum swung today, and I thought, instead of my own body, of Maurice's. I thought of certain lines life had put on his face, as personal as lines of his writing. I thought of a new scar on his shoulder that wouldn't have been there if once he hadn't tried to protect another man's body from a falling wall. He didn't tell me why he was in hospital those three days; Henry told me. That scar was part of his character as much as his jealousy. And so I thought, do I want that body to be vapour—mine, yes, but his? And I knew I wanted that scar to exist through all eternity. But could my vapour love that scar? Then I began to want my body that I hated, but only because it could love that scar. We can love with our minds, but can we love only with our minds? Love extends itself all the time, so that we can even love with our senseless nails; we love even with our clothes, so that a sleeve can feel a sleeve.

Richard's right, I thought; we have invented the resurrection of the body because we do need our own bodies, and immediately I admitted that he was right and that this was a fairy tale we tell each other for comfort, I no longer felt any hate of those statues. They were like bad coloured pictures in Hans Andersen; they were like bad poetry, but somebody had needed to write them, somebody who wasn't so proud that he hid them rather than expose his foolishness. I walked up the church, looking at them one after the other. In front of the worst of all— I don't know who she was—a middle-aged man was praying. He had put his bowler hat beside him, and in the bowler hat, wrapped in newspaper, were some sticks of celery.

And of course on the altar there was a body too—such a familiar body, more familiar than Maurice's, that it had never struck me before as a body with all the parts of a body, even the parts the loincloth concealed. I remembered one in a Spanish church I had visited with Henry, where the blood ran down in scarlet paint from the eyes and the hands. It had sickened me. Henry wanted me to admire the twelfth-century pillars, but I was sick, and I wanted to get out into the open air. I thought, these people love cruelty. A vapour couldn't shock you with blood and cries.

When I came out into the plaza I said to Henry, "I can't bear all these painted wounds." Henry was very reasonable—he's always reasonable. He said, "Of course it's a very materialistic faith. A lot of magic—"

"Is magic materialistic?" I asked.

"Yes. 'Eye of newt and toe of frog, finger of birth-strangled babe.' You can't have anything more materialistic than that. In the Mass they still believe in transsubstantiation."

I knew all about that, but I had an idea that it had more or less died out at the Reformation—except for the poor, of course. Henry put me right—how often has Henry rearranged my muddled thoughts! "Materialism isn't only an attitude for the poor," he said. "Some of the finest brains have been materialist—Pascal, Newman. So subtle in some directions; so crudely superstitious in others. One day we may know why. It may be a glandular deficiency."

So today I looked at that material body on that material cross, and I wondered, how could the world have nailed a vapour there? A vapour, of course, felt no pain and no pleasure. It was only my superstition that imagined it could answer my prayers. Dear God, I had said; I should have said, Dear Vapour. I had said, I hate you; but can one hate a vapour? I could hate that figure on the cross with its claim to my gratitude—"I've suffered this for you"—but a vapour— And yet Richard believed in less even than a vapour. He hated a fable, he fought against a fable, he took a fable seriously. I couldn't hate Hansel and Gretel, I couldn't hate their sugar house as he hated the legend of Heaven. When I was a child I could hate the wicked queen in Snow White, but Richard didn't hate his fairy-tale devil. The devil didn't exist, and God didn't exist, but all his hatred was for the good fairy tale, not for the wicked one. Why? I looked up at that over-familiar body, stretched in imaginary pain, the head drooping like a man asleep. I thought, sometimes I've hated Maurice, but would I have hated him if I hadn't loved him too? O God, if I could really hate you, what would that mean?

Am I a materialist after all? I wondered. Have I some glandular deficiency, that I am so uninterested in the really important unsuperstitious things and causes, like the Charity Commission and the cost-of-living index and better calories for the working class? Am I a materialist because I believe in the independent existence of that man with the bowler, the metal of that cross, these hands I can't pray with? Suppose God did exist, suppose he was a body like that. What's wrong in believing that his body existed as much as mine? Could anybody love him or hate him if he hadn't got a body? I can't love a vapour that was Maurice. That's coarse, that's beastly, that's materialist, I know—but why shouldn't I be beastly and coarse and materialist? I walked out of the church in a flaming rage and, in defiance of Henry and all the reasonable and the detached, I did what I had seen people do in Spanish churches: I dipped my finger in the so-called holy water and made a kind of cross on my forehead.

January 10, 1946.

I couldn't stand the house tonight, so I walked out into the rain. I remembered the time when I had stuck my nails into my palms, and I didn't know it, but You moved in the pain. I said, "Let him be alive," not believing in You, and my disbelief made no difference to You. You took it into Your love and accepted it like an offering, and tonight the rain soaked through my coat and my clothes and into my skin, and I shivered with the cold, and it was for the first time as though I nearly loved You. I walked under Your windows in the rain and I wanted to wait under them all night only to show that after all I might learn to love and I wasn't afraid of the desert any longer because You were there. I came back into the house, and there was Maurice with Henry. It was the second time You had given him back; the first time I had hated You for it, and You'd taken my hate, like You'd taken my disbelief, into Your love, keeping them to show me later, so that we could both laugh— as I have sometimes laughed at Maurice, saying, "Do you remember how stupid we were? . . ."

January 18, 1946.

I was having lunch with Maurice for the first time in two years—I had telephoned and asked him to meet me—and my bus got held up in the traffic at Stockwell, and I was ten minutes late. I felt the fear for a moment I always felt in the old days, that something would happen to spoil the day, that he would be angry with me. But I had no desire to get in first now with my anger. Like a lot of other things, the capacity for anger seems dead in me. I wanted to see him and ask him about Henry. Henry's been odd lately. It was strange of him to go out and drink in a pub with Maurice. Henry only drinks at home or at his club. I thought he might have talked to Maurice. Strange if he's worried about me. There's never been less cause for worry since we married first. But when I was with Maurice there didn't seem any other reason to be with him except to be with him. I found out nothing about Henry. Every now and then he tried to hurt me and he succeeded because he was really hurting himself, and I can't bear to watch him hurting himself.

Have I broken that old promise, lunching with Maurice? A year ago I would have thought so, but I don't think so now. I was very literal in those days because I was afraid, because I didn't know what it was all about, because I had no trust in love. We lunched at Rule's, and I was happy just being with him. Only for a little I was unhappy, saying good-bye above the grating. I thought he was going to kiss me again, and I longed for it, and then a fit of coughing took me and the moment passed. I knew, as he walked away, he was thinking all kinds of untrue things and he was hurt by them, and I was hurt because he was hurt.

I wanted to cry unobserved, and I went to the National Portrait Gallery, but it was students' day, there were too many people, so I went back to Maiden Lane and into the church that's always too dark to look at your neighbour. I sat there. It was quite empty except for me and for a little man who came in and prayed quietly in a pew behind. I remembered the first time I had been in one of those churches and how I had hated it. I didn't pray. I had prayed once too often. I said to God, as I might have said to my father, if I could ever have remembered having one, Dear God, I'm tired.

February 3, 1946.

Today I saw Maurice, but he didn't see me. He was on his way to the Pontefract Arms, and I trailed behind him. I had spent an hour in Cedar Road—a long dragging hour, trying to follow poor Richard's arguments and only getting from them a sense of inverted belief. Could anyone be so serious, so argumentative, about a legend? When I understood anything at all, it was some strange fact I didn't know that hardly seemed to me to help his case—like the evidence that there had been a man called Christ. I came out feeling tired and hopeless. I had gone to him to rid me of a superstition, but every time I went his fanaticism fixed the superstition deeper. I was helping him, but he wasn't helping me. Or was he? For an hour I had hardly thought of Maurice, but then suddenly there he was, crossing the end of the street.

I followed him all the way, keeping him in sight. So many times we had been together to the Pontefract Arms. I knew which bar he'd go to, what he'd order. Should I go in after him, I wondered, and order mine and see him turn, and everything would start over again? The mornings would be full of hope because I could telephone him as soon as Henry left, and there would be evenings to look forward to when Henry warned me that he would be home late. And perhaps now I would leave Henry. I'd done my best. I had no money to bring Maurice, and his books brought in little more than enough to keep himself; but on typing alone, with me to help, we should save fifty pounds a year. I don't fear poverty. Sometimes it's easier to cut your coat to fit the cloth than to lie on the bed you've made.

I stood at the door and watched him go up to the bar. If he turns round and sees me, I told God, I'll go in; but he didn't turn round. I began to walk home, but I couldn't keep him out of my mind. For nearly two years we had been strangers. I hadn't known what he was doing at any particular hour of the day, but now he was a stranger no longer because I knew as in the old days where he was. He would have one more beer and then he would go back to the familiar room to write. The habits of his day were still the same, and I loved them as one loves an old coat. I felt protected by his habits. I never want strangeness.

And I thought, how happy I can make him and how easily. I longed again to see him laugh with happiness.

Henry was out. He had had a lunch engagement that made him late at the office, and he had telephoned to say that he wouldn't be in till seven. I would wait till half-past six and then I would telephone Maurice. I would say, I am coming for tonight and all the other nights. I'm tired of being without you. I would pack the large blue suitcase and the small brown one. I would take enough clothes for a month's holiday. Henry was civilized, and by the end of a month the legal aspects would have been settled, the immediate bitterness would be over, and anything else I needed from the house could be fetched at leisure. There wouldn't be much bitterness; it wasn't as though we were still lovers. Marriage had become friendship, and the friendship, after a little, could go on the same as before.

Suddenly I felt free and happy. I'm not going to worry about you any more, I said to God as I walked across the Common, whether you exist or whether you don't exist, whether you gave Maurice a second chance or whether I imagined everything. Perhaps this is the second chance I asked for him. I'm going to make him happy; that's my second vow, God, and stop me if you can, stop me if you can.

I went upstairs to my room and I began to write to Henry. "Darling Henry," I wrote, but that sounded hypocritical. Dearest was a lie, and so it had to be like an acquaintance, "Dear Henry." So "Dear Henry," I wrote, "I'm afraid this will be rather a shock to you, but for the last five years I've been in love with Maurice Bendrix. For two years nearly we haven't seen each other or written, but it doesn't work. I can't live happily without him, so I've gone away. I know I haven't been much of a wife for a long time, and I haven't been a mistress at all since June 1944, so everybody's the worse off all round. I thought once I could just have this love affair and it would peter slowly and contentedly out, but it hasn't worked that way. I love Maurice more than I did in 1939. I've been childish, I suppose, but now I realize that sooner or later one has to choose or one makes a mess in all directions. Good-bye. God bless you." I crossed out "God bless you" very deeply so that it couldn't be read. It sounded smug, and anyway Henry doesn't believe in God. Then I wanted to put "Love," but the word sounded unsuitable, although I knew it was true. I do love Henry in my shabby way.

I put the letter in an envelope and marked it "Very Personal." I thought that would warn Henry not to open it in anybody's presence—for he might bring home a friend, and I didn't want his pride hurt. I pulled out the suitcase and began to pack, and then I suddenly thought, where did I put the letter? I found it at once, but then I thought, suppose in my hurry I forget to put it in the hall, and Henry waits and waits for me to come home. So I carried it downstairs to put it in the hall. My packing was nearly done—only an evening dress to fold—and Henry wasn't due for another half-hour.

I had just put the letter on the hall table on top of the afternoon's post when I heard a key in the door. I snatched it up again, I don't know why, and then Henry came in. He looked ill and harassed. He said, "Oh, you're here?" and walked straight by me and into his study. I waited a moment and then I followed. I thought,

I'll have to give him the letter now; it's going to need more courage. When I opened the door I saw him sitting in his chair by the fire he hadn't bothered to light, and he was crying.

"What is it, Henry?" I asked him.

He said, "Nothing. I've got a bad headache, that's all."

I lit the fire for him. I said, "I'll get you some veganin."

"Don't bother," he said. "It's better already."

"What sort of a day have you had?"

"Oh, much the same as usual. A bit tiresome."

"Who was your lunch date?"

"Bendrix."

"Bendrix?" I said.

"Why not Bendrix? He gave me lunch at his club. A horrible lunch."

I came behind him and put my hand on his forehead. It was an odd thing to be doing just before leaving him forever. He used to do that to me when we were first married and I had terrible nervous headaches because nothing was going right. I forgot for a moment that I would only pretend to be cured that way. He put up his own hand and pressed mine harder against his forehead. "I love you," he said. "Do you know that?"

"Yes," I said. I could have hated him for saying it; it was like a claim. If you really loved me, I thought, you'd behave like any other injured husband. You'd get angry, and your anger would set me free.

"I can't do without you," he said. Oh, yes, you can, I wanted to protest. It will be inconvenient, but you can. You changed your newspaper once and you soon got used to it. These are words, conventional words of a con-

ventional husband. and they don't mean anything at all.
Then I looked up at his face in the mirror, and he was
crying still.

"Henry," I said, "what's wrong?"

"Nothing. I told you."

"I don't believe you. Has something happened at the
office?"

He said with unfamiliar bitterness, "What could happen there?"

"Did Bendrix upset you in some way?"

"Of course not. How could he?"

I wanted to take away his hand, but he held it there. I
was afraid of what he'd say next, of the unbearable bur-
dens he was laying on my conscience. Maurice would be
home by now; if Henry hadn't come in, I would have
been with him in five minutes. I would have seen happiness instead of misery. If you don't see misery you don't
believe in it. You can give anyone pain from a distance.
Henry said, "My dear, I haven't been much of a husband."

"I don't know what you mean," I said.

"I'm dull for you. My friends are dull. We no longer—
you know—do anything together."

"It has to stop sometime," I said, "in any marriage.
We are good friends." That was to be my escape line.
When he agreed I would give him the letter, I would tell
him what I was going to do, I would walk out of the
house. But he missed his cue, and I'm still here, and the
door has closed again against Maurice. Only I can't put
the blame on God this time. I closed the door myself.

Henry said, "I can never think of you as a friend. You

can do without a friend." And he looked back at me from the mirror and he said, "Don't leave me, Sarah. Stick it a few more years. I'll try—" But he couldn't think himself what he'd try. Oh, it would have been better for both of us if I'd left him years ago, but I can't hit him when he's there, and now he'll always be there because I've seen what his misery looks like.

I said, "I won't leave you. I promise." Another promise to keep, and when I had made it I couldn't bear to be with him any more. He'd won, and Maurice had lost, and I hated him for his victory. Would I have hated Maurice for his? I went upstairs and tore up the letter so small nobody could put it together again, and I kicked the suitcase under the bed because I was too tired to start unpacking, and I started writing this down. Maurice's pain goes into his writing; you can hear the nerves twitch through his sentences. Well, if pain can make a writer, I'm learning, Maurice, too. I wish I could talk to you just once. I can't talk to Henry. I can't talk to anyone. Dear God, let me talk.

Yesterday I bought a crucifix, a cheap ugly one because I had to do it quickly. I blushed when I asked for it. Somebody might have seen me in the shop. They ought to have opaque glass in their doors like rubber-goods shops. When I lock the door of my room I can take it out from the bottom of my jewel case. I wish I knew a prayer that wasn't me, me, me. Help *me*. Let *me* be happier. Let *me* die soon. Me, me, me.

Let me think of the strawberry mark on Richard's cheek. Let me see Henry's face with the tears falling Let me forget me. Dear God, I've tried to love and I've made such a hash of it. If I could love You, I'd know how to love them. I believe the legend. I believe You were born. I believe You died for us. I believe You are God. Teach me to love. I don't mind my pain. It's their pain I can't stand. Let my pain go on and on, but stop theirs. Dear God, if only You could come down from Your cross for a while and let me get up there instead. If I could suffer like You, I could heal like You.

February 4, 1946.

Henry took a day off work. I don't know why. He gave me lunch, and we went to the National Gallery and we had an early dinner and went to the theatre. He was like a parent coming down to the school and taking the child out. But he's the child.

February 5, 1946.

Henry's planning a holiday abroad for us in the spring. He can't make up his mind between the châteaux of the Loire or Germany, where he could make a report on the morale of the Germans under bombing. I never want the spring to come. There I go again. I want. I don't want. If I could love You, I could love Henry. God was made man. He was Henry with his astigmatism, Richard with his strawberry mark, not only Maurice. If I could love a leper's sores, couldn't I love the boringness of Henry? But I'd turn from the leper if he were here, I suppose, as I shut myself away from Henry. I want the dramatic always. I imagine I'm ready for the pain of

Your nails, and I can't stand twenty-four hours of maps and Michelin guides. Dear God, I'm no use. I'm still the same bitch and fake. Clear me out of the way.

February 6, 1940.

Today I had a terrible scene with Richard. He was telling me of the contradictions in the Christian churches, and I was trying to listen but I wasn't succeeding very well, and he noticed it. He said to me suddenly, "What do you come here for?" And before I could catch myself I said, "To see you."

"I thought you came to learn," he said, and I told him that's what I meant.

I knew he didn't believe me, and I thought his pride would be hurt and he'd be angry, but he wasn't angry at all. He got up from his chintzy chair and came and sat with me on the chintzy sofa on the side where his cheek wouldn't show. He said, "It's meant a lot to me, seeing you every week." And then I knew that he was going to make love to me. He put his hand on my wrist and asked, "Do you like me?"

"Yes, Richard, of course," I said, "or I wouldn't be here."

"Will you marry me?" he asked, and his pride made him ask it as though he were asking whether I'd take another cup of tea.

"Henry might object," I said, trying to laugh it off.

"Nothing will make you leave Henry?" And I thought angrily, if I haven't left him for Maurice, why the hell should I be expected to leave him for you?

"I'm married."

"That doesn't mean anything to me or you."

"Oh, yes, it does," I said. I had to tell him sometime. "I believe in God," I said, "and all the rest. You've taught me to. You and Maurice."

"I don't understand."

"You've always said the priests taught you to disbelieve. Well, it can work the other way too."

He looked at his beautiful hands; he had those left. He said very slowly, "I don't care what you believe. You can believe the whole silly bag of tricks for all I care. I love you, Sarah."

"I'm sorry," I said.

"I love you more than I hate all that. If I had children by you, I'd let you pervert them."

"You shouldn't say that."

"I'm not a rich man. It's the only bribe I can offer, giving up my faith."

"I'm in love with somebody else, Richard."

"You can't love him much if you feel bound by that silly vow."

I said drearily, "I've done my best to break it, but it didn't work."

"Do you think me a fool?"

"Why should I?"

"To expect you to love a man with this." He turned his crinkled scarlet cheek towards me. "You believe in God," he said. "That's easy. You are beautiful. You have no complaint, but why should I love a God who gives a child this?"

"Dear Richard," I said, "there's nothing so very bad—" I shut my eyes and put my mouth against the mark.

I felt sick for a moment because I fear deformity, and he sat quiet and let me kiss him, and I thought, I am kissing pain, and pain belongs to You as happiness never does. I love You in Your pain. I could almost taste metal and salt in the skin, and I thought, how good You are. You might have killed us with happiness, but You let us be with You in pain.

I felt him move abruptly away and I opened my eyes. He said, "Good-bye."

"Good-bye, Richard."

"Don't come back," he said. "I can't bear your pity."

"It's not pity."

"I've made a fool of myself."

I went away. It wasn't any good staying. I couldn't tell him I envied him, carrying the mark of pain around with him like that, seeing You in the glass every day instead of this dull human thing we call beauty.

February 10, 1946.

I have no need to write to You or talk to You—that's how I began a letter to You a little time ago, and I was ashamed of myself and I tore it up because it seemed such a silly thing to write a letter to You, who know everything before it comes into my mind. Did I ever love Maurice as much before I loved You? Or was it really You I loved all the time? Did I touch You when I touched him? Could I have touched You if I hadn't touched him first, touched him as I never touched Henry, anybody? And he loved me and touched me as he never did with any other woman. But was it me he loved, or You? For he hated in me the things You hate. He was on Your side all the time without knowing it. You willed our separation, but he willed it too. He worked for it with his anger and his jealousy, and he worked for it with his love. For he gave me so much love and I gave him so much love that soon there wasn't anything left when we'd finished but You. For either of us. I might have taken a lifetime spending a little love at a time, doling it out here and there, on this man and that. But even the first time, in the hotel near Paddington, we spent all we had. You were there, teaching us to squander, like You taught the rich man, so that one day we might have nothing left except this love of You. But You are too good to me. When I ask You for pain, You give me peace. Give it him too. Give him my peace—he needs it more.

February 12, 1946.

Two days ago I had such a sense of peace and quiet and love. Life was going to be happy again, but last night I dreamed I was walking up a long staircase to meet Maurice at the top. I was still happy because when I reached the top of the staircase we were going to make love. I called to him that I was coming, but it wasn't Maurice's voice that answered; it was a stranger's that boomed like a foghorn warning lost ships, and scared me. I thought, he's let his flat and gone away and I don't know where he is, and going down the stairs again the water rose beyond my waist and the hall was thick with mist. Then I woke up. I'm not at peace any more. I just want him like I used to in the old days. I want to be eating sandwiches with him. I want to be drinking with him in a bar. I'm tired and I don't want any more pain. I want Maurice. I want ordinary corrupt human love. Dear God, You know I want to want Your pain, but I don't want it now. Please take it away for a while and give it me another time.

BOOK FOUR

1

I COULDN'T READ any more. Over and over again I had
skipped when a passage hurt me too much. I had wanted
to discover about Dunstan, though I hadn't wanted to
discover that much; but now I had read on, it slipped far
back in time, like a dull date in history. It wasn't of present importance. The entry I was left with was an entry
only one week old. "I want Maurice. I want ordinary corrupt human love."

It's all I can give you, I thought. I don't know about
any other kind of love, but if you think I've squandered
all of that you're wrong. There's enough left for our two
lives. And I thought of that day when she had packed
her suitcase and I sat working here, not knowing that
happiness was so close. I was glad that I hadn't known
and I was glad that I knew. I could act now. Dunstan
didn't matter. The air-raid warden didn't matter. I went
to the telephone and dialled her number.

The maid answered. I said, "This is Mr. Bendrix. I
want to speak to Mrs. Miles." She told me to hold on.
I felt breathless, as though I were at the end of a long race,
as I waited for Sarah's voice, but the voice that came was
the maid's, telling me that Mrs. Miles was out. I don't
know why I didn't believe her. I waited five minutes
and then, with my handkerchief stretched tight over the
mouthpiece, I rang again.

"Is Mr. Miles in?"

"No, sir."

"Could I speak to Mrs. Miles then? This is Sir William Mallock."

There was only a very short pause before Sarah replied. "Good evening. This is Mrs. Miles."

"I know," I said. "I know your voice, Sarah."

"You. I thought—"

"Sarah," I said, "I'm coming to see you."

"No, please no. Listen, Maurice. I'm in bed. I'm speaking from there now."

"All the better."

"Don't be a fool, Maurice. I mean I'm ill."

"Then you'll have to see me. What's the matter, Sarah?"

"Oh, nothing. A bad cold. Listen, Maurice." She spaced her words slowly like a governess, and it angered me. "Please—don't—come—I—can't—see—you."

"I love you, Sarah, and I'm coming."

"I won't be here. I'll get up." I thought, if I run, it will take me only four minutes across the Common; she can't dress in that time. "I'll tell the maid not to let anybody in."

"She's not got the build of a chucker-out. And I'd have to be chucked out, Sarah."

"Please, Maurice, I'm asking you. I haven't asked anything of you for a long time."

"Except one lunch."

"Maurice, I'm not awfully fit. I just can't see you today. Next week—"

"There've been a terrible lot of weeks. I want to see you now. This evening."

"Why, Maurice?"

"You love me."

"How do you know?"

"Never mind. I want to ask you to come away with me."

"But, Maurice, I can answer you on the phone just as well. The answer's no."

"I can't touch you by telephone, Sarah."

"Maurice, my dear, please. Promise you won't come."

"I'm coming."

"Listen, Maurice. I'm feeling awfully sick. And the pain's bad tonight. I don't want to get up."

"You don't have to."

"I swear I'll get up and dress and leave the house, unless you promise—"

"This is more important to both of us, Sarah, than a cold."

"Please, Maurice, please. Henry will be home soon."

"Let him be." I rang off.

It was a worse night than the one when I had met Henry, a month before. This time it was halfway to snow, and the edged drops seemed to slash their way in through the buttonholes of one's raincoat; they obscured the lamps on the Common, so that it was impossible to run, and I can't run fast anyway because of my leg. I wished I had brought my wartime torch with me, for it must have taken eight minutes for me to reach the house on the north side. I was just stepping off the pavement to cross when the door opened and Sarah came out. I thought with happiness, I have her now. I knew with absolute certainty that before the night was out we should

have slept together again. And once that had been re-
newed anything might happen. I had never known her
before and I had never loved her so much. The more we
know the more we love, I thought. I was back in the territory of trust.

She was in too much of a hurry to see me, across the
wide roadway through the sleet. She turned to the left
and walked rapidly away. I thought, she will need somewhere to sit down, and then I have her trapped. I followed twenty yards behind, but she never looked back.
She skirted the Common, past the pond and the bombed
bookshop, as though she was making for the tube. Well,
if it was necessary, I was prepared to talk to her even in
a crowded train. She went down the tube stairs and up to
the booking office, but she had no bag with her, and,
when she felt in her pockets, no loose money either—
not even the three halfpence that would have enabled her
to travel up and down till midnight. Up the stairs again,
and across the road where the trams run. One earth had
been stopped, but another had obviously come to mind.
I was triumphant. She was afraid, but she wasn't afraid
of me, she was afraid of herself and what was going to
happen when we met. I felt I had won the game already,
and I could afford to feel a certain pity for my victim. I
wanted to say to her, Don't worry, there's nothing to
fear, we'll both be happy soon, the nightmare's nearly
over.

And then I lost her. I had been too confident and I had
allowed her too big a start. She had crossed the road
twenty yards ahead of me—I was delayed again by my

bad leg, coming up the stairs—a tram ran between, and she was gone. She might have turned left down the High Street or gone straight ahead down Park Road, but I couldn't see her. I wasn't very worried; if I didn't find her today I would the next. Now I knew the whole absurd story of the vow, now I was certain of her love, I was assured of her. If two people loved, they slept together; it was a mathematical formula, tested and proved by human experience.

There was an A.B.C. in the High Street, and I tried that. She wasn't there. Then I remembered the church at the corner of Park Road, and I knew at once that she had gone there. I followed, and sure enough, there she was, sitting in one of the side aisles, close to a pillar and a hideous statue of the Virgin. She wasn't praying. She was just sitting there with her eyes closed. I saw her only by the light of the candles before the statue, for the whole place was very dark. I sat down behind her, like Mr. Parkis, and waited. I could have waited years, now that I knew the end of the story. I was cold and wet and very happy. I could even look with charity towards the altar and the figure dangling there. She loves us both, I thought, but if there is to be a conflict between an image and a man, I know who will win. I could put my hand on her thigh or my mouth on her breast; he was imprisoned behind the altar and couldn't move to plead his cause.

Suddenly she began to cough, her hand pressed to her side. I knew she was in pain and I couldn't leave her alone in pain. I came and sat beside her and put my hand on her knee while she coughed. I thought, if only one had a touch that could heal. When the fit was over she said, "Please won't you let me be."

"I'll never let you be," I said.

"What's come over you, Maurice? You weren't like that the other day at lunch."

"I was bitter. I didn't know you loved me."

"Why do you think I do?" she asked, but she let my hand rest on her knee. I told her then how Mr. Parkis had stolen her diary; I didn't want any lies between us now.

"It wasn't a good thing to do," she said.

"No."

She began to cough again and afterwards, in her exhaustion, she leaned her shoulder against me.

"My dear," I said, "it's all over now. The waiting, I mean. We're going away together."

"No," she said.

I put my arm round her and touched her breast. "This is where we begin again," I said. "I've been a bad lover, Sarah. It was the insecurity that did it. I didn't trust you. I didn't know enough about you. But I'm secure now."

She said nothing but she still leaned against me. It was like an assent. I said, "I'll tell you how it had better be. Go back home and lie in bed for a couple of days—you don't want to travel with a cold like that. I'll ring up every day and see how you are. When you are well enough I'll come over and help you pack. We won't stay here. I have a cousin in Dorset who has an empty cottage I can use. We'll stay there a few weeks and rest. I'll be able to finish my book. We can face the lawyers afterwards. We need a rest, both of us. I'm tired and I'm sick to death of being without you, Sarah."

"Me too." She spoke so low that I wouldn't have heard the phrase if I had been a stranger to it, but it was like a signature tune that had echoed through all our relationship, from the first love-making in the Paddington hotel. "Me too," for loneliness, griefs, disappointments, pleasures, and despairs—the claim to share everything.

"Money's going to be short," I said, "but not too short. I've been commissioned to do a life of General Gordon, and the advance is enough to keep us for three months comfortably. By that time I can hand in the novel and get an advance on that. Both books will be out this year, and they should keep us till another's ready. I can work, with you there. You know any moment now I'm going to come through. I'll be a vulgar success yet, and you'll hate it, and I'll hate it, but we'll buy things and be extravagant, and it will be fun because we'll be together."

Suddenly I realized she was asleep. Exhausted by her flight, she had fallen asleep against my shoulder as so many times, in taxis, in buses, on a park seat. I sat still and let her be. There was nothing to disturb her in the dark church. The candles flapped around the Virgin, and there was nobody else there. The slowly growing pain in my upper arm where her weight lay was the greatest pleasure I had ever known.

Children are supposed to be influenced by what you whisper to them in sleep, and I began to whisper to Sarah, not loud enough to wake her, hoping that the words would drop hypnotically into her unconscious mind. "I love you, Sarah," I whispered. "Nobody has ever loved you as much before. We are going to be happy. Henry won't mind, except in his pride, and pride soon heals. He'll find himself a new habit to take your place; perhaps he'll collect Greek coins. We are going away, Sarah, we are going away. Nobody can stop it now. You love me, Sarah." And I fell silent as I began to wonder whether I ought to buy a new suitcase. Then she woke, coughing.

"I've been asleep," she said.

"You must go home now, Sarah. You're cold."

"It isn't home, Maurice," she said. "I don't want to go away from here."

"It's cold."

"I don't mind the cold. And it's dark. I can believe anything in the dark."

"Just believe in us."

"That's what I meant." She shut her eyes again, and, looking up at the altar, I thought with triumph, almost as though he were a living rival, you see, these are the arguments that win. And gently I moved my fingers across her breast.

"You're tired, aren't you?" I asked.

"Very tired."

"You shouldn't have run away from me like that."

"It wasn't you I was running from." She moved her shoulder. "Please, Maurice, go now."

"You ought to be in bed."

"I will be soon. I don't want to go back with you. I just want to say good-bye here."

"Promise you won't stay long."

"I promise."

"And you'll telephone to me?"

She nodded, but, looking down at her hand where it lay in her lap like something thrown away, I saw that she had her fingers crossed. I asked her with suspicion, "You are telling me the truth?" I uncrossed her fingers with mine and said, "You aren't planning to escape me again?"

"Maurice, dear Maurice," she said, "I haven't got the strength." She began to cry, thrusting her fists into her eyes as a child does.

"I'm sorry," she said. "Just go away. Please, Maurice, have a bit of mercy."

One gets to the end of badgering and contriving; I couldn't go on, with that appeal in my ears. I kissed her on the tough and knotty hair and, coming away, I found her lips, smudgy and salt, on the corner of my mouth. "God bless you," she said, and I thought, that's what she crossed out in her letter to Henry.

One says good-bye to another's good-bye—unless one is Smythe—and it was an involuntary act when I repeated her blessing back to her, but, turning as I left the church, and seeing her huddled there at the edge of the candle-light like a beggar come in for warmth, I could imagine a God blessing her or a God loving her. When I began to write our story down I thought I was writing a record of hate, but somehow the hate has got mislaid, and all I know is that in spite of her mistakes and her unreliability she was better than most. It's just as well that one of us should believe in her; she never did in herself.

The next few days I had to make a great effort to be sensible. I was working for both of us now. In the morning I set myself a minimum of seven hundred and fifty words on the novel, but usually I managed to get a thousand done by eleven o'clock. It's astonishing, the effect of hope; the novel that had dragged all through the last year ran towards its end. I knew that Henry left for work around nine-thirty, and the most likely hour for her to telephone was between then and twelve-thirty. Henry had started coming home for lunch, so Parkis had told me; there was no chance of her telephoning again before three. I would revise my day's work and do my letters until twelve-thirty, and then I was released, however gloomily, from expectation. Until two-thirty I could put in time at the British Museum Reading Room, making notes for the life of General Gordon. I couldn't absorb myself in reading and note-taking as I could in writing the novel, and the thought of Sarah came between me and the missionary life in China. Why had I been invited to write this biography? I often wondered. They would have done better to have chosen an author who believed in Gordon's God. I could appreciate the obstinate stand at Khartoum, the hatred of the safe politicians at home, but the Bible on the desk belonged to another world of thought from mine, the world of love. Well, the publisher was Jewish, and perhaps he half hoped that my cynical treatment of Gordon's Christianity would cause a *succès de scandale*. I had no intention of pleasing him;

this God was also Sarah's God, and I was going to throw no stones at any phantom she believed she loved. I hadn't during that period any hatred of her God, for hadn't I in the end proved stronger?

One day while I was eating my sandwiches, onto which my indelible pencil somehow always got transferred, a familiar voice greeted me from the desk opposite in a tone hushed out of respect to our fellow workers. "I hope all goes well now, sir, if you'll forgive the personal intrusion."

I looked over the back of my desk at the unforgettable moustache. "Very well, Parkis, thank you. Have an illicit sandwich?"

"Oh, no, sir, I couldn't possibly—"

"Come now. Imagine it's on expenses." Reluctantly he took one and, opening it up, remarked with a kind of horror as though he had accepted a coin and found it gold, "It's real ham."

"My publisher sent me a tin from America."

"It's too good of you, sir."

"I still have your ash tray, Parkis," I whispered, because my neighbour had looked angrily up at me.

"It's of sentimental value only," he whispered back.

"How's your boy?"

"A little bilious, sir."

"I'm surprised to find you here. Work? You aren't watching one of us, surely?" I couldn't imagine that any of the dusty inmates of the reading room—the men who wore hats and scarves indoors for warmth, the Indian who was painfully studying the complete works of George Eliot, or the man who slept every day with his

head laid beside the same pile of books—could be con-
cerned in any drama of sexual jealousy.

"Oh, no, sir. This isn't work. It's my day off, and the
boy's back at school today."

"What are you reading?"

"The *Times* Law Reports, sir. Today I'm on the Russell case. They give a kind of background to one's work,
sir. Open up vistas. They take one away from the daily
petty detail. I knew one of the witnesses in this case, sir.
We were in the same office once. Well, he's gone down to
history as I never shall now."

"Oh, you never know, Parkis."

"One does know, sir. That's the discouraging thing.
The Bolton case was as far as I'll ever get. The law that
forbade the evidence in divorce cases being published was
a blow to men of my calling. The judge, sir, never men-
tions us by name, and he's very often prejudiced against
the profession."

"It had never struck me," I said with sympathy.

Even Parkis could awake a longing. I could never
see him without the thought of Sarah. I went home in
the tube with hope for company and, sitting at home,
in dying expectation of the telephone bell's ringing, I saw
my companion depart again; it wouldn't be today. At
five o'clock I dialled the number, but as soon as I heard
the ringing tone I replaced the receiver; perhaps Henry
was back early, and I couldn't speak to Henry now,
for I was the victor, since Sarah loved me and Sarah
wanted to leave him. But a delayed victory can strain the
nerves as much as a prolonged defeat.

Eight days passed before the telephone rang. It wasn't

the time of day I expected, for it was before nine o'clock in the morning, and when I said, "Hullo," it was Henry who answered.

"Is that Bendrix?" he asked. There was something very queer about his voice, and I wondered, has she told him?

"Yes. Speaking."

"An awful thing's happened. You ought to know. Sarah's dead."

How conventionally we behave at such moments. I said, "I'm terribly sorry, Henry."

"Are you doing anything tonight?"

"No."

"I wish you'd come over for a drink. I don't fancy being alone."

BOOK FIVE

I

I STAYED the night with Henry. It was the first time I had slept in Henry's house. They had only one guest room, and Sarah was there (she had moved into it a week before so as not to disturb Henry with her cough), so I slept on the sofa in the drawing room where we had made love. I didn't want to stay the night, but he begged me to.

We must have drunk a bottle and a half of whisky between us. I remember Henry's saying, "It's strange, Bendrix, how one can't be jealous about the dead. She's only been dead a few hours, and yet I wanted you with me."

"You hadn't so much to be jealous about. It was all over a long time ago."

"I don't need that kind of comfort now, Bendrix. It was never over with either of you. I was the lucky man. I had her all those years. Do you hate me?"

"I don't know, Henry. I thought I did, but I don't know."

We sat in his study with no light on. The gas fire was not turned high enough for us to see each other's faces, so that I could tell when Henry wept only by the tone of his voice. The Discus Thrower aimed at both of us from the darkness. "Tell me how it happened, Henry."

"You remember that night I met you on the Common. Three weeks ago, or four, was it? She got a bad cold that night. She wouldn't do anything about it. I never even knew it had reached her chest. She never told anybody those sort of things." And not even her diary, I thought. There had been no word of sickness there. She hadn't had the time to be ill in.

"She took to her bed in the end," Henry said, "but nobody could have kept her there, and she wouldn't have a doctor—she never believed in them. She got up and went out a week ago. God knows where or why. She said she needed exercise. I came home first and found her gone. She didn't get in till nine, soaked through worse than the first time. She must have been walking about for hours in the rain. She was feverish all night, talking to somebody; I don't know who—it wasn't you or me, Bendrix. I made her see a doctor after that. He said if she'd had penicillin a week earlier he'd have saved her."

There wasn't anything for either of us to do but pour out more whisky. I thought of the stranger I had paid Parkis to track down; the stranger had certainly won in the end. No, I thought, I don't hate Henry. I hate you if you exist. I remembered what she'd said to Richard Smythe, that I had taught her to believe. I couldn't for the life of me tell how, but to think what I had thrown away made me hate myself too. Henry said, "She died at four this morning. I wasn't there. The nurse didn't call me in time."

"Where's the nurse?"

"She finished her job off very tidily. She had another urgent case and left before lunch."

"I wish I could be of use to you."

"You are, just sitting here. It's been an awful day, Bendrix. You know, I've never had a death to deal with.

I always assumed I'd die first, and Sarah would have known what to do—if she's stayed with me that long. In a way it's a woman's job, like having a baby."

"I suppose the doctor helped."

"He's awfully rushed this winter. He rang up an undertaker. I wouldn't have known where to go. We've never had a trade directory. But a doctor can't tell me what to do with her clothes—the cupboards are full of them. Compacts, scents—one can't just throw things away. If only she had a sister—" He suddenly stopped because the front door opened and closed, just as it had on that other night when he had said, "The maid," and I had said, "It's Sarah." We listened to the footsteps of the maid going upstairs. It's extraordinary how empty a house can be with three people in it. We drank our whisky, and I poured another. "I've got plenty in the house," Henry said. "Sarah found a new source—" He stopped again. She stood at the end of every path. There wasn't any point in trying to avoid her even for a moment. I thought, why did you have to do this to us? If she hadn't believed in you she would be alive now, we should have been lovers still. It was sad and strange to remember that I had been dissatisfied with the situation. I would have shared her now happily with Henry.

I said, "And the funeral?"

"Bendrix, I don't know what to do. Something very puzzling happened. When she was delirious—of course she wasn't responsible—the nurse told me that she kept on asking for a priest. At least she kept on saying, 'Father, Father,' and it couldn't have been her own. She never knew him. Of course the nurse knew we weren't Catholics. She was quite sensible. She soothed her down. But I'm worried, Bendrix."

I thought with anger and bitterness, you might have left poor Henry alone. We have got on for years without you. Why should you suddenly start intruding into all situations like a strange relation returned from the Antipodes?

Henry said, "If one lives in London cremation's the easiest thing. Until the nurse said that to me, I'd been planning to have it done at Golders Green. The undertaker rang up the crematorium. They can fit Sarah in the day after tomorrow."

"She was delirious," I said. "You don't have to take what she said into account."

"I wondered whether I ought to ask a priest about it. She kept so many things quiet. For all I know she may have become a Catholic. She's been so strange lately."

"Oh, no, Henry. She didn't believe in anything, any more than you or I." I wanted her burned up, I wanted to be able to say, Resurrect that body if you can; my jealousy had not finished, like Henry's, with her death. It was as if she were alive still, in the company of a lover she had preferred to me. How I wished I could send Parkis after her to interrupt their eternity.

"You are quite certain?"

"Quite certain, Henry." I've got to be careful, I thought. I mustn't be like Richard Smythe, I mustn't hate, for if I were really to hate I would believe, and if I were to believe, what a triumph for you and her. This is play-acting, talking about revenge and jealousy; it's just something to fill the brain with, so that I can forget the absoluteness of her death. A week ago I had only to say to her, "Do you remember that first time together and how I hadn't got a shilling for the meter?" and the scene would be there for both of us. Now it was there for me only. She had lost all our memories forever, and it was as though by dying she had robbed me of part of myself. I was losing my individuality. It was the first stage of my own death, the memories dropping off like gangrened limbs.

"I hate all this fuss of prayers and gravediggers, but if Sarah wanted it I'd try to get it arranged."

"She chose her wedding in a registry office," I said. "She wouldn't want her funeral to be in a church."

"No, I suppose that's true, isn't it?"

"Registration and cremation," I said, "they go together." And in the shadow Henry lifted his head and peered towards me as though he suspected my irony.

"Let me take it all out of your hands," I suggested, just as in the same room, by the same fire, I had suggested visiting Mr. Savage for him.

"It's good of you, Bendrix." He drained the last of the whisky into our glasses, very carefully and evenly.

"Midnight," I said. "You must get some sleep. If you can."

"The doctor left me some pills." But he didn't want to be alone yet. I knew exactly how he felt, for I too, after a day with Sarah, would postpone for as long as I could the loneliness of my room.

"I keep on forgetting she's dead," Henry said. And I had experienced that too, all through 1945—the bad year —forgetting when I woke that our love affair was over, that the telephone might carry any voice except hers. She had been as dead then as she was dead now. For a month or two this year a ghost had pained me with hope, but the ghost was laid, and the pain would be over soon. It would die a little more every day, but how I longed to retain it. As long as one suffers one lives.

"Go to bed, Henry."

"I'm afraid of dreaming about her."

"You won't if you take the doctor's pills."

"Would you like one, Bendrix?"

"No."

"You wouldn't, would you, stay the night? It's filthy outside."

"I don't mind the weather."

"You'd be doing me a great favour."

"Of course I'll stay."

"I'll bring down some sheets and blankets."

"Don't bother, Henry." But he was gone. I looked at the parquet floor and I remembered the exact timbre of her cry. On the desk where she wrote her letters was a clutter of objects, and every object I could interpret like a code. She hasn't even thrown away that pebble, I thought. We laughed at its shape, and there it still is, like a paper-weight. What would Henry make of it, and the miniature bottle of a liqueur none of us cared for, and the piece of glass polished by the sea, and the small wooden rabbit I had found in Nottingham? Should I take all these objects away with me? They would go into the waste-paper basket otherwise, when Henry at last got around to clearing up—but could I bear their company?

I was looking at them when Henry came in, burdened

with blankets. "I had forgotten to say, Bendrix, if there's anything you want to take—in memory. I don't think she left a will."

"It's kind of you."

"I'm grateful now to anybody who loved her."

"I'll take this stone if I may."

"She kept the oddest things. I've brought you a pair of my pajamas, Bendrix."

Henry had forgotten to bring a pillow, and, lying with my head on a cushion, I imagined I could smell her scent. I wanted things I should never have again; there was no substitute. I couldn't sleep. I pressed my nails into my palms as she had done with hers, so that the pain might prevent my brain from working, and the pendulum of my desire swung tiringly to and fro, the desire to forget and to remember, to be dead and to keep alive a while longer. And then at last I slept. I was walking up Oxford Street and I was worried because I had to buy a present, and all the shops were full of cheap jewellery, glittering under the concealed lighting. Now and then I thought I saw something beautiful and I approached the glass, but when I saw the jewel close it was as factitious as all the others—perhaps a hideous green bird with scarlet eyes meant to give the effect of rubies. Time was short, and I hurried from shop to shop. Then out of one of the shops came Sarah, and I knew that she would help me. "Have you bought something, Sarah?" "Not here," she said, "but they have some lovely little bottles farther on."

"I haven't time," I begged her. "Help me. I've got to find something, for tomorrow's the birthday."

"Don't worry," she said. "Something always turns up. Don't worry." And suddenly I didn't worry. Oxford Street extended its boundaries into a great grey misty field, my feet were bare, and I was walking in the dew, alone, and, stumbling in a shallow rut, I woke, still hearing, "Don't worry," like a whisper lodged in the ear, a summer sound belonging to childhood.

At breakfast time Henry was still asleep, and the maid whom Parkis had suborned brought coffee and toast in to me on a tray. She drew the curtains, and the sleet had changed blindingly to snow. I was still bleary with sleep and the contentment of my dream, and I was surprised to see her eyes red with old tears. "Is anything the matter, Maud?" I asked, and it was only when she put the tray down and walked furiously out that I came properly awake to the empty house and the empty world. I went up and looked in at Henry. He was still in the depths of drugged sleep, smiling like a dog, and I envied him. Then I went down and tried to eat my toast.

A bell rang, and I heard the maid leading somebody upstairs—something to do with the undertaking, I supposed, because I could hear the door of the guest room open. He was seeing her dead; I had not, but I had no wish to, any more than I would have wished to see her in another man's arms. Some men may be stimulated that way; I am not. Nobody was going to make me pimp for death. I drew my mind together and I thought, now that everything is really over, I have got to begin again. I have fallen in love once; it can be done again. But I was unconvinced. It seemed to me that I had given away all the sex I had.

Another bell. What a lot of business was going on in the house while Henry slept. This time Maud came to me. She said, "There's a gentleman below asking for Mr. Miles, but I don't like to wake him."

"Who is he?"

"He's that friend of Mrs. Miles," she said, and for the only time admitted her share in our shabby collaboration.

"You'd better show him up," I said. I felt very superior to Smythe now, sitting in Sarah's drawing room, wearing Henry's pajamas, knowing so much about him while he knew nothing about me. He looked at me with confusion and dripped snow onto the parquet. I said, "We met once. I'm a friend of Mrs. Miles."

"You had a small boy with you."

"That's right."

"I came to see Mr. Miles," he said.

"You've heard the news?"

"That's why I came."

"He's asleep. The doctor gave him pills. It's been a bad shock to all of us," I added foolishly. He was staring round the room; in Cedar Road. coming out of nowhere, she had been as dimensionless, I suppose, as a dream. But this room gave her thickness; it was Sarah too. The snow mounted slowly on the sill like mould from a spade. The room was being buried like Sarah.

He said, "I'll come back," and turned drearily away, so that his livid cheek was turned on me. I thought, that was where her lips rested. She could always be snared by pity.

He repeated stupidly, "I came to see Mr. Miles and say how sorry—"

"It's more usual on these occasions to write."

"I thought I might be of some use," he said weakly.

"You don't have to convert Mr. Miles."

"Convert?" he asked, ill at ease and bewildered.

"To the fact that there's nothing left of her. The end. Annihilation."

He broke suddenly out. "I wanted to see her, that's all."

"Mr. Miles doesn't even know you exist. It's not very considerate of you, Smythe, to come here."

"When is the funeral?"

"Tomorrow at Golders Green."

"She wouldn't have wanted that," he said and took me by surprise.

"She didn't believe in anything, any more than you claim you do."

He said, "Don't any of you know? She was becoming a Catholic."

"Nonsense."

"She wrote to me. She'd made up her mind. Nothing I could have said would have done any good. She was beginning—instruction. Isn't that the word they use?"

So she still had secrets, I thought. She had never put that in her journal, any more than she had put her sickness. How much more was there to discover? The thought was like despair.

"That was a shock for you, wasn't it?" I jeered at him, trying to transfer my pain.

"Oh, I was angry, of course. But we can't all believe the same things."

"That's not what you used to claim."

He looked at me as though he were puzzled by my enmity. He said, "Is your name Maurice by any chance?"

"It is."

"She told me about you."

"And I read about you. She made fools of us both."

"I was unreasonable." He touched the strawberry mark with his finger. He said, "Don't you think I could see her?" and I heard the heavy boots of the undertaker's man coming downstairs.

"She's lying upstairs. The first door on the left."

"If Mr. Miles—"

"You won't wake him."

I had put on my clothes by the time he came down again. He said, "Thank you."

"Don't thank me. I don't own her any more than you do."

"I've got no right to ask," he said, "but I wish you'd—you loved her, I know." He added as though he were swallowing a bitter medicine, "She loved you."

"What are you trying to say?"

"I wish you'd do something for her."

"For her?"

"Let her have her Catholic funeral. She would have liked it."

"What earthly difference does it make?"

"I don't suppose any for her. But it always pays us to be generous."

"And what have I to do with it?"

"She always said that her husband had a great respect for you."

He was turning the screw of absurdity too far. I

wished to shatter the deadness of this buried room with laughter. I sat down on the sofa and began to shake with it. I thought of Sarah dead upstairs and Henry asleep with a silly smile on his face, and the lover with the strawberry mark discussing the funeral with the lover who had employed Mr. Parkis to sprinkle his doorbell with powder. The tears ran down my cheeks as I laughed. Once in the blitz I saw a man laughing outside his house, where his wife and child were buried.

"I don't understand," Smythe said. He held his right fist closed as though he were prepared to defend himself. There was so much that neither of us understood. Pain was like an inexplicable explosion, throwing us together. "I'll be going," he said, and reached for the doorknob with his left hand. A strange idea occurred to me because I had no reason to believe he was left-handed.

"You must forgive me," I said. "I'm rattled. We're all rattled." I held out my hand to him; he hesitated, and touched it with his left. "Smythe," I said, "what have you got there? Did you take anything from her room?" He opened his hand and showed a scrap of hair. "That's all," he said.

"You hadn't any right."

"Oh, she doesn't belong to anybody now," he said, and suddenly I saw her for what she was—a piece of refuse waiting to be cleared away; if you needed a bit of hair you could take it, or trim her nails if nail trimmings had value to you. Like a saint's her bones could be divided up—if anybody required them. She was going to be burned soon, so why shouldn't everybody have what he wanted first? What a fool I had been during three years to imagine that in any way I had possessed her. We are possessed by nobody, not even by ourselves.

"I'm sorry," I said.

"Do you know what she wrote to me?" Smythe asked. "It was only four days ago." And I thought with sadness that she had had time to write to him but not to telephone to me. "She wrote, 'Pray for me.' Doesn't it seem odd, asking *me* to pray for her?"

"What did you do?"

"Oh," he said, "when I heard she was dead I prayed."

"Did you know any prayers?"

"No."

"It doesn't seem right praying to a God you don't believe in."

I followed him out of the house; there was no point in remaining till Henry woke. Sooner or later he had to face being on his own, just as I had. I watched Smythe jerking his way across the Common ahead of me, and I thought, a hysterical type. Disbelief could be a product of hysteria just as much as belief. The wet of the snow, where the passage of many people had melted it, worked through my soles and reminded me of the dew in my dream, but when I tried to remember her voice saying, "Don't worry," I found I had no memory for sounds. I couldn't imitate her voice. I couldn't even caricature it; when I tried to remember it, it was anonymous—just any woman's voice. The process of forgetting her had set in. We should keep gramophone records as we keep photographs.

I came up the broken steps into the hall. Nothing but the stained glass was the same as that night in 1944.

Nobody knows the beginning of anything. Sarah had really believed that the end began when she saw my body. She would never have admitted that the end had started long before: the fewer telephone calls for this or that inadequate reason, the quarrels I began with her because I had realized the danger of love's ending. We had begun to look beyond love, but it was only I who was aware of the way we were being driven. If the bomb had fallen a year earlier, she wouldn't have made that promise. She would have torn her nails trying to release me. When we get to the end of human beings we have to delude ourselves into a belief in God, like a gourmet who demands more complex sauces with his food. I looked at the hall, clear as a cell, hideous with green paint, and I thought, she wanted me to have a second chance, and here it is: the empty life, odourless, antiseptic, the life of a prison. And I accused her as though her prayers had really worked the change—what did I do to you that you had to condemn me to life? The stairs and banisters creaked with newness all the way upstairs. She had never walked up them. Even the repairs to the house were part of the process of forgetting. It needs a God outside time to remember when everything changes. Did I still love or did I only regret love?

I came into my room, and on the desk lay a letter from Sarah.

She had been dead for twenty-four hours and unconscious for longer than that. How could a letter take so long across a strip of common? Then I saw that she had put my number wrong, and a little of the old bitterness seeped out. She wouldn't have forgotten my number two years ago.

There was so much pain at the idea of seeing her writing that I nearly held the letter to the gas fire, but curiosity can be stronger than pain. It was written in pencil, I suppose because she was writing in bed.

"Dearest Maurice," she wrote, "I meant to write to you the other night after you had gone away, but I felt rather sick when I got home, and Henry fussed about me. I'm writing instead of telephoning. I can't telephone and hear your voice go queer when I say I'm not going to come away with you. Because I'm not going to come away with you, Maurice, dearest Maurice. I love you and I can't see you again. I don't know how I'm going to live in this pain and longing and I'm praying to God all the time that He won't be hard on me, that He won't keep me alive. Dear Maurice, I want to have my cake and eat it like everybody else. I went to a priest two days ago before you rang me up and I told him I wanted to be a Catholic. I told him about my promise and about you. I said, I'm not really married to Henry any more. We don't sleep together—not since the first year with you. And it wasn't really a marriage, I said; you couldn't call a registry office a wedding. I asked him, couldn't I be a Catholic and marry you? I knew you wouldn't mind going through a service. Every time I asked him a question I had such hope; it was like opening the shutters in a new house and looking for the view, and every window just faced a blank wall. No, no, no, he said, I couldn't marry you, I couldn't go on seeing you, not if I was going to be a Catholic. I thought, to hell with the whole lot of them, and I walked out of the room where I was seeing him, and I slammed the door to show what I thought of priests. They are between us and God, I thought; God has more mercy; and then I came out of the church and saw the crucifix they have there, and I thought, of course He's got mercy, only it's such an odd sort of mercy, it sometimes looks like punishment. Maurice, my dearest, I've got a foul headache and I feel like death. I wish I weren't as strong as a horse. I don't want to live without you, and I know one day I shall meet you on the Common and then I won't care a damn about Henry or God or anything. But what's the good, Maurice? I believe there's a God—I believe the whole bag of tricks; there's nothing I don't believe; they could subdivide the Trinity into a dozen parts and I'd believe. They could dig up records that proved Christ had been invented by Pilate to get himself promoted, and I'd believe just the same. I've caught belief like a disease. I've fallen into belief like I fell in love. I've never loved before as I love you, and I've never believed in anything before as I believe now. I'm sure. I've never been sure before about anything. When you came in at the door with the blood on your face, I became sure. Once and for all. Even though I didn't know it at the time. I fought belief for longer than I fought love, but I haven't any fight left.

"Maurice, dear, don't be angry. Be sorry for me, but don't be angry. I'm a phony and a fake, but this isn't phony or fake. I used to think I was sure about myself and what was right and wrong, and you taught me not to be sure. You took away all my lies and self-deceptions like they clear a road of rubble for somebody to come along it, somebody of importance, and now He's come, but you cleared the way yourself. When you write you try to be exact, and you taught me to want the truth, and you told me when I wasn't telling the truth. 'Do you really think that,' you'd say, 'or do you only think you think it?' So you see it's all your fault, Maurice, it's all your fault. I pray to God He won't keep me alive like this."

There wasn't any more. She seemed to have had a knack of getting her prayers answered even before they were spoken, because hadn't she started dying that night when she came in out of the rain and found me with Henry? If I were writing a novel I would end it here; a novel, I used to think, has to end somewhere, but I'm beginning to believe my realism has been at fault all these years, for nothing now in life ever seems to end. Chemists tell you nothing is ever completely destroyed, and mathematicians tell you that if you halve each pace in crossing a room, you will never reach the opposite wall, so what an optimist I would be if I thought that this story ended here. Only, like Sarah, I wish I weren't as strong as a horse.

II

I was late for the funeral. I had gone into town to meet a man called Waterbury who was going to write an article on my work in one of the little reviews. I tossed up whether I'd see him or not; I knew too well the pompous phrases of his article, the buried significances he would discover of which I was unaware, and the faults I was tired of facing. Patronizingly, in the end, he would place me probably a little above Maugham because Maugham is popular and I have not yet committed that crime—not yet, but although I retain a little of the exclusiveness of unsuccess, the little reviews, like wise detectives, can scent it on its way.

Why did I ever trouble to toss up? I didn't want to meet Waterbury and certainly I didn't want to be written about. For I have come to an end of my interest in work now; no one can please me much with praise or hurt me with blame. When I began that novel about the civil servant I was still interested, but when Sarah left me I recognized my work for what it was—as unimportant a drug as cigarettes to get one through the weeks and years. If we are extinguished by death, as I still try to believe, what point is there in leaving some books behind any more than bottles, clothes, or cheap jewellery? And if Sarah is right, how unimportant all the importance of art is. I tossed up, I think, simply from loneliness. I hadn't anything to do before the funeral; I wanted to fortify myself with a drink or two—one may cease to care about

one's work, but one never ceases to care about conven-
tions, and a man must not break down in public.

Waterbury was waiting in a sherry bar off Tottenham
Court Road. He wore black corduroy trousers and
smoked cheap cigarettes, and he had with him a girl
much taller and better-looking than he was who wore
the same kind of trousers and smoked the same cigarettes. She was very young and she was called Sylvia, and
one knew that she was on a long course of study that had
only begun with Waterbury; she was at the stage of imitating her teacher. I wondered where, with those looks,
those alert good-natured eyes and hair the gold of illu-
minations, she would end. Would she even remember
Waterbury in ten years and the bar off Tottenham Court
Road? I felt sorry for him. He was so proud now, so
patronizing to both of us, but he was on the losing side.
Why, I thought, catching her eye over my glass at a particularly fatuous comment of his about the stream of
consciousness, even now I could get her from him. His
articles were bound in paper, but my books were bound
in cloth. She knew she could learn more from me. And
yet, poor devil, poor pimply devil, he had the nerve to
snub her when occasionally she made a simple human
unintellectual comment. I wanted to warn him of the
empty future, but instead I took another glass and said,
"I can't stay long. I have to go to a funeral in Golders
Green."

"A funeral in Golders Green!" Waterbury exclaimed.
"How like one of your own characters. It would have to
be Golders Green, wouldn't it?"

"I didn't choose the spot."

"Life imitating art."

"Is it a friend?" Sylvia asked with sympathy, and Waterbury glared at her for her irrelevance.

"Yes."

I could see that she was speculating—man? woman? what kind of a friend?—and it pleased me. For I was a human being to her and not a writer, a man whose friends died and who attended their funerals, who felt pleasure and pain, who might even need comfort, not just a skilled craftsman whose work has greater sympathy perhaps than Mr. Maugham's, though of course we cannot rank it as high as . . .

"What do you think of Forster?" Waterbury asked.

"Forster? Oh, I'm sorry. I was just wondering how long it took to Golders Green."

"You ought to allow forty minutes," Sylvia said. "You have to wait for an Edgware train."

"Forster," Waterbury repeated irritably.

"You'll have to take a bus from the station," Sylvia said.

"Really, Sylvia, Bendrix hasn't come here to talk about how to get to Golders Green."

"I'm sorry, Peter, I just thought—"

"Count six before thinking, Sylvia," Waterbury said. "And now can we get back to E. M. Forster?"

"Need we?" I asked.

"It would be interesting, as you belong to such different schools."

"Does he belong to a school? I didn't even know that I did. Are you writing a textbook?"

Sylvia smiled, and he saw the smile. I knew from that

moment he would grind sharp the weapon of his trade, but it didn't matter to me. Indifference and pride look very much alike, and he probably thought I was proud. I said, "I ought to be going."

"But you've only been here five minutes. It's really important to get this article right."

"It's really important for me not to be late at Golders Green."

"I don't see why."

Sylvia said, "I'm going as far as Hampstead myself. I'll put you on your way."

"You never told me," Waterbury said with suspicion.

"You know I always see my mother on Wednesdays."

"Today's Tuesday."

"Then I needn't go tomorrow."

"It's very good of you," I said. "I'd like your company."

"You used the stream of consciousness in one of your books," Waterbury said with desperate haste. "Why did you abandon the method?"

"Oh, I don't know. Why does one change a flat?"

"Did you feel it was a failure?"

"I feel that about all my books. Well, good-bye."

"I'll send you a copy of the article," he said as though he were uttering a threat.

"Thanks."

"Don't be late, Sylvia. There's the Bartok programme on the Third at six-thirty."

We went out together into the debris of Tottenham Court Road. I said, "Thank you for breaking up the party."

"Oh, I knew you wanted to get away," she said.

"What's your other name?"

"Black."

"Sylvia Black," I said. "It's a good combination. Almost too good."

"Was it a great friend?"

"Yes."

"A woman?"

"Yes."

"I'm sorry," she said, and I had the impression that she meant it. She had a lot to learn in the way of books and music and how to dress and talk, but she would never have to learn humanity. She came down with me into the crowded tube, and we strap-hung side by side. Feeling her against me, I was reminded of desire. Would that always be the case now—not desire, but only the reminder of it? She turned to make way at Goodge Street for a newcomer, and I was aware of her thigh against my leg as one is aware of something that has happened a long time ago.

"This is the first funeral I've ever been to," I said to make conversation.

"Are your father and mother alive, then?"

"My father is. My mother died when I was away at school. I thought I'd get a few days' holiday, but my father thought it would upset me, so I made nothing out of it at all. Except I was let off prep the night the news arrived."

"I wouldn't like to be cremated," she said.

"You'd prefer worms?"

"Yes, I would."

Our heads were so close together that we could talk

without raising our voices, but we couldn't look at each other because of the press of people. I said, "It wouldn't matter to me one way or the other," and wondered immediately why I had bothered to lie, because it *had* mattered, it must have mattered, for it was I in the end who had persuaded Henry against burial.

III

On the afternoon before, Henry had wavered. He had telephoned, asking me to come over. It was odd how close we had become with Sarah gone. He depended on me now much as before he had depended on Sarah—I was somebody familiar about the house. I even pretended to wonder whether he would ask me to share the house when once the funeral was over, and what answer I would give him. From the point of view of forgetting Sarah, there was nothing to choose between the two houses: she had belonged to both.

He was still hazy with his drugs when I arrived, or I might have had more trouble with him. A priest sat rigidly on the edge of an armchair in the study, a man with a sour gaunt face, one of the Redemptorists, probably, who served up Hell on Sundays in the dark church where I had last seen Sarah. He had obviously antagonized Henry from the start, and that had helped.

"This is Mr. Bendrix, the author," Henry said. "Father Crompton. Mr. Bendrix was a great friend of my wife's." I had the impression that Father Crompton knew that already. His nose ran down his face like a buttress, and I thought, perhaps this is the very man who slammed the door of hope on Sarah.

"Good afternoon," Father Crompton said with such ill-will that I felt the bell and the candle were not far away.

"Mr. Bendrix has helped me a great deal with all the arrangements," Henry explained.

"I would have been quite ready to take them off your hands if I had known."

There had been a time when I hated Henry. My hatred now seemed petty. Henry was a victim as much as I was a victim, and the victor was this grim man in the silly collar. I said, "You could hardly have done that, surely. You disapprove of cremation."

"I could have arranged a Catholic burial."

"She wasn't a Catholic."

"She had expressed the intention of becoming one."

"Is that enough to make her one?"

Father Crompton produced a formula. He laid it down like a bank note. "We recognize the baptism of desire." It lay there between us, waiting to be picked up. Nobody made a move. Father Crompton said, "There's still time to cancel your arrangements." He repeated, "I will take everything off your hands"—repeated it in a tone of admonition as though he were addressing Lady Macbeth and promising her some better process of sweetening her hands than the perfumes of Arabia.

Henry said suddenly, "Does it really make much difference? Of course, I'm not a Catholic, Father, but I can't see—"

"She would have been happier."

"But why?"

"The Church offers privileges, Mr. Miles, as well as responsibilities. There are special Masses for our dead. Prayers are regularly said. We remember our dead," he added, and I thought angrily, how do you remember them? Your theories are all right. You preach the importance of the individual. Our hairs are all numbered, you say, but I can feel her hair on the back of my hand; I can remember the fine dust of hair at the base of the spine as she lay face down on my bed. We remember our dead too, in our way.

Watching Henry weaken, I lied firmly, "We've absolutely no reason to believe she would have become a Catholic."

Henry began, "Of course the nurse did say—" But I interrupted him. "She was delirious at the end."

Father Crompton said, "I would never have dreamed of intruding on you, Mr. Miles, without serious reason."

"I had a letter from Mrs. Miles, written less than a week before she died," I told him. "How long is it since you saw her?"

"About the same time. Five or six days ago."

"It seems very odd to me that she didn't even mention the subject in her letter."

"Perhaps, Mr.—Mr. Bendrix, you hadn't her confidence."

"Perhaps, Father, you jump a little too quickly to conclusions. People can be interested in your faith, ask questions about it, without necessarily wishing to become Catholics." I went quickly on to Henry, "It would be absurd to alter everything now. Directions have been given. Friends have been invited. Sarah was never a fanatic. She would be the last to want any inconvenience caused for the sake of a whim. After all," I drove on, fixing my eyes on Henry, "it will be a perfectly Christian ceremony. Not that Sarah was even a Christian. We saw no signs of it anyway. But you could always give Father Crompton money for a Mass."

"it isn't necessary. I said one this morning." He made a movement with his hands in his lap, the first break in his rigidity; it was like watching a strong wall shift and lean after a bomb had fallen. "I shall remember her every day in my Mass," he said.

Henry said with relief, as though that settled matters, "Very good of you, Father," and moved a cigarette box.

"It seems an odd and impertinent thing to say to you, Mr. Miles, but I don't think you realize what a good woman your wife was."

"She was everything to me," Henry said.

"A great many people loved her," I said.

Father Crompton turned his eyes on me like a head-master who hears an interruption at the back of the class from some snotty youngster.

"Perhaps not enough," he said.

"Well," I said, "to go back to what we were discussing. I don't think we can alter things now, Father. It would cause a great deal of talk, too. You wouldn't like talk, would you, Henry?"

"No. Oh, no."

"There's the insertion in the *Times*. We should have to put in a correction. People notice that kind of thing. It would cause comment. After all, you aren't unknown, Henry. Then telegrams would have to be sent. A lot of people will have had wreaths delivered already to the crematorium. You see what I mean, Father."

"I can't say that I do."

' What you ask is not reasonable."

"You seem to have a very strange set of values, Mr. Bendrix."

"But surely you don't believe cremation affects the resurrection of the body, Father?"

"Of course I don't. I've told you my reasons already. If they don't seem strong enough to Mr. Miles, there's no more to be said." He got up from his chair—and what an ugly man he was. Sitting down, he had at least the appearance of power, but his legs were too short for his body, and he rose unexpectedly small. It was as if he had suddenly moved a long way off.

Henry said, "If you'd come a little sooner, Father—please don't think—"

"I don't think anything wrong of you, Mr. Miles."

"Of me perhaps, Father?" I asked with deliberate impertinence.

"Oh, don't worry, Mr. Bendrix. Nothing you can do will affect her now." I suppose the Confessional teaches a man to recognize hate. He held his hand out to Henry and turned his back on me. I wanted to say to him, You're wrong about me. It's not Sarah I hate. And you are wrong about Henry too. He is the corrupter, not me. I wanted to defend myself—"I loved her"—for surely in the Confessional they learn to recognize that emotion too.

IV

"Hampstead's the next stop," Sylvia said.

"You've got to get out to see your mother?"

"I could come on to Golders Green and show you the way. I don't usually see her today."

"It would be an act of charity," I said.

"I think you'll have to take a taxi if you are to be on time."

"I suppose it doesn't really matter missing the opening lines."

She saw me to the courtyard of the station, and then she wanted to go back. It seemed strange to me that she had taken so much trouble. I have never seen any qualities in me for a woman to like, and now less than ever. Grief and disappointment are like hate; they make men ugly with self-pity and bitterness. And how selfish they make us too. I had nothing to give Sylvia; I would never be one of her teachers; but because I was afraid of the next half-hour, the faces that would be spying on my loneliness, trying to detect from my manner what my relations with Sarah had been, who had left whom, I needed her beauty to support me.

"But I can't come in these clothes," she protested when I begged for her company. I could tell how pleased she was that I wanted her with me. I knew I could have taken her from Waterbury there and then. His sands had already run out. If I chose he would listen to Bartok alone.

"We'll stand at the back," I said. "You might be just a stranger walking round."

"At least they are black," she said, referring to her trousers. In the taxi I let my hand lie on her leg like a promise, but I had no intention of keeping my promise. The crematorium tower was smoking, and the water lay in half-frozen puddles on the gravel walks. A lot of strangers came by—from a previous cremation, I supposed; they had the brisk cheerful air of people who have left a dull party and can now "go on."

"It's this way," Sylvia said.

"You know the place very well?"

"Daddy was done here two years ago."

As we reached the chapel everyone was leaving. Waterbury's questions about the stream of consciousness had delayed me just too long. I had an odd conventional stab of grief—I hadn't, after all, "seen the last" of Sarah, and I thought dully, so it was her smoke that was blowing over the suburban gardens. Henry came blindly out alone; he had been crying and he didn't see me. I knew nobody else, except Sir William Mallock, who wore a top hat. He gave me a look of disapproval and hurried on. There were half a dozen men with the air of civil servants. Was Dunstan there? It wasn't very important. Some wives had accompanied their husbands. They at least were satisfied with the ceremony—you could almost tell it from their hats. The extinction of Sarah had left every wife safer.

"I'm so sorry," Sylvia said.

"It wasn't your fault."

I thought, if we could have embalmed her, they would never have been safe. Even her dead body would have provided a standard to judge them by.

Smythe came out and splashed quickly away among the puddles, speaking to nobody. I heard a woman say, "The Carters have asked us the week end of the tenth."

"Would you like me to go?" Sylvia asked.

"No, no," I said, "I like having you around."

I went to the door of the chapel and looked in. The runway to the furnace was empty for the moment, but, as the old wreaths were being carried out, new ones were being carried in. An elderly woman was kneeling incongruously in prayer like an actor from another scene caught by the unexpected raising of a curtain. A familiar voice behind me said, "It's a sad pleasure to see you here, sir, where bygones are always bygones."

"You've come, Parkis!" I exclaimed.

"I saw the announcement in the *Times,* sir, so I asked Mr. Savage's permission to take the afternoon off."

"Do you always follow your people as far as this?"

"She was a very fine lady, sir," he said reproachfully. "She asked me the way once in the street, not knowing of course my reason for being around. And at the cocktail party she handed me a glass of sherry."

"South African sherry?" I asked him miserably.

"I wouldn't know, sir, but the way she did it—oh, there weren't many like her. My boy too— He's always speaking about her."

"How is your boy, Parkis?"

"Not well, sir. Not at all well. Very violent stomach aches."

"You've seen a doctor?"

"Not yet, sir. I believe in leaving things to nature. Up to a point."

I looked round at the groups of strangers who had all known Sarah. I said, "Who are these people, Parkis?"

"The young lady I don't know, sir."

"She's with me."

"I beg your pardon. Sir William Mallock is the one on the horizon, sir."

"I know him."

"The gentleman who's just avoided a puddle, sir, is the head of Mr. Miles's department."

"Dunstan?"

"That's the name, sir."

"What a lot you know, Parkis." I had thought jealousy was quite dead; I had thought myself willing to share her with a world of men if only she could be alive again, but the sight of Dunstan woke for a few seconds the old hatred. "Sylvia," I called, as though Sarah could hear me, "are you dining anywhere tonight?"

"I promised Peter—"

"Peter?"

"Waterbury."

"Forget him."

Are you there? Are you watching me, I said to Sarah. See how I can get on without you. It isn't so difficult, I said to her. My hatred could believe in her survival; it was only my love that knew she existed no more than a dead bird.

A new funeral was gathering, and the woman by the rail rose in confusion at the sight of the strangers coming in. She had nearly been caught up in the wrong cremation.

"I suppose I could phone."

Hate lay like boredom over the evening ahead. I had committed myself. Without love I would have to go through the gestures of love. I felt the guilt before I had committed the crime, the crime of drawing the innocent into my own maze. The act of sex may be nothing, but when you reach my age you learn that at any time it may prove to be everything. I was safe, but who could tell to what neurosis in this child I might appeal? At the end of the evening I would make love clumsily, and my very clumsiness, even my impotence if I proved impotent, might do the trick; or I would make love expertly, and my experience too might involve her. I implored Sarah, Get me out of this, get me out of it, for her sake, not mine.

Sylvia said, "I could say my mother was ill." She was ready to lie; it was the end of Waterbury. Poor Waterbury. With that first lie we should become accomplices. She stood there in her black trousers, among the frozen puddles, and I thought this is where a whole long future may begin. I implored Sarah, Get me out of it. I don't want to begin it all again and injure her. I'm incapable of love. Except of you, except of you; and the grey old woman swerved towards me, crackling the thin ice. "Are you Mr. Bendrix?" she asked.

"Yes."

"Sarah told me—" she began, and while she hesitated a wild hope came to me that she had a message to deliver, that the dead could speak. "You were her best friend; she often told me."

"I was one of them."

"I'm her mother." I hadn't even remembered her mother was alive; in those years there had always been so much to talk about between us that whole areas of both our lives were blank like an early map, to be filled in later.

She said, "You didn't know about me, did you?"

"As a matter of fact—"

"Henry didn't like me. It made it rather awkward, so I kept away." She spoke in a calm reasonable way, and yet the tears came out of her eyes with an effect of independence. The men and their wives had all cleared off; the strangers picked their way among the three of us, going into the chapel. Only Parkis lingered, thinking, I suppose, that he might yet be of use to me in supplying further information, but he kept his distance, knowing, as he would have said, his place.

"I've a great favour to ask of you," Sarah's mother said. I tried to remember her name—Cameron? Chandler? it began with a C. "I came up today from Great Missenden in such a hurry—" She wiped the tears out of her eyes indifferently, as if she were using a washcloth. Bertram, I thought, that was the name, Bertram.

"Yes, Mrs. Bertram," I said.

"And I forgot to change the money into my black bag."

"Anything I can do."

"If you would lend me a pound, Mr. Bendrix. You see, I have to get some dinner in town before I leave. It's early closing at Great Missenden." And she wiped her eyes again as she spoke. Something about her reminded me of Sarah: a matter-of-factness in her grief, perhaps an ambiguity. Had she "touched" Henry once too often?

I said, "Have an early dinner with me."

"You wouldn't want to be bothered."

"I loved Sarah," I said.

"So did I."

I went back to Sylvia and explained. "That's her mother. I'll have to give her dinner. I'm sorry. Can I ring you up and make another date?"

"Of course."

"Are you in the book?"

"Waterbury is," she said gloomily.

"Next week."

"I'd love it." She put her hand out and said, "Goodbye." I could tell that she knew it was one of those things that had missed the moment. Thank God, it didn't matter—a mild regret and curiosity as far as the tube station, a cross word to Waterbury over the Bartok. Turning back to Mrs. Bertram, I found myself speaking again to Sarah: You see, I love you. But love had not the same conviction of being heard as hate had.

As we approached the crematorium gates, I noticed that Parkis had slipped away. I hadn't seen him go. He must have realized that now I had no more need of him.

Mrs. Bertram and I had dinner at the Isola Bella. I didn't want to go anywhere I had ever been with Sarah, and of course at once I began to compare this restaurant with all the others we had visited together. Sarah and I never drank Chianti, and now the act of drinking it reminded me of that fact. I might as well have had our favourite claret, I couldn't have thought of her more. Even vacancy was crowded with her.

"I didn't like that service," Mrs. Bertram said.

"I'm sorry."

"It was so inhuman. Like a conveyor belt."

"It seemed suitable. There were prayers, after all."

"That clergyman—was he a clergyman?"

"I didn't see him."

"He talked about the Great All. I didn't understand for a long time. I thought he was saying the Great Auk." She began to drip again into her soup. She said, "I nearly laughed, and Henry saw me. I could see that he put that against my account."

"You don't hit it off?"

"He's a very mean man," she said. She wiped her eyes with her napkin and then she rattled her spoon fiercely in the soup, stirring up the noodles. "I once had to borrow ten pounds from him because I'd come to London to stay and forgot my bag. It could happen to anybody."

"Of course it could."

"I always pride myself on not having a debt in the world."

Her conversation was like the tube system; it moved in circles and loops. I began by the coffee to notice the recurring stations: Henry's meanness, her own financial integrity, her love for Sarah, her dissatisfaction with the funeral service, the Great All—that was where certain trains went on to Henry.

"It was so funny," she said. "I didn't want to laugh. Nobody loved Sarah more than I did." How we all always make that claim and are angered when we hear it on another's tongue. "But Henry wouldn't understand that. He's a cold man."

I made a great effort to switch the points. "I don't see what other kind of service we could have had."

"Sarah was a Catholic," she said. She took her glass of port and swallowed half of it in a gulp.

"Nonsense," I said.

"Oh," Mrs. Bertram said, "she didn't know it herself."

Suddenly, inexplicably, I felt fear, like a man who has committed the all-but-perfect crime and watches the first unexpected crack in the wall of his deception. How deep does the crack go? Can it be plugged in time?

"I don't understand a thing you are saying."

"Sarah never told you I was a Catholic—once?"

"No."

"I wasn't very much of one. You see, my husband hated the whole business. I was his third wife, and when I got cross with him the first year I used to say we weren't properly married. He was a mean man," she added mechanically.

"Your being a Catholic doesn't make Sarah one."

She took another gulp at her port. She said, "I've never told another soul. I think I'm a bit tight. Do you think I'm tight, Mr. Bendrix?"

"Of course not. Have another port."

While we were waiting for it, she tried to switch the conversation, but I brought her relentlessly back. "What did you mean, Sarah was a Catholic?"

"Promise you won't tell Henry."

"I promise."

"We were abroad one time in Normandy. Sarah was just over two. My husband used to go to Deauville—so he said, but I knew he was seeing his first wife. I got so cross. Sarah and I went for a walk along the sands. Sarah kept on wanting to sit down, but I'd give her a rest and then we'd walk a little. I said, 'This is a secret between you and me, Sarah.' Even then she was good at secrets, if she wanted to be. I was scared, I can tell you, but it was a good revenge, wasn't it?"

"Revenge? I don't understand you very well, Mrs. Bertram."

"On my husband, of course. It wasn't only because of his first wife. I told you, didn't I, that he wouldn't let me be a Catholic? Oh, there were such scenes if I tried to go to Mass, so I thought, Sarah's going to be a Catholic, and he won't know, and I shan't tell him unless I get really angry."

"And didn't you?"

"He went and left me a year after that."

"So you were able to be a Catholic again?"

"Oh, well, I didn't *believe* much, you see. And then I married a Jew, and he was difficult too. They tell you Jews are awfully generous. Don't you believe it. Oh, he was a mean man."

"But what happened on the beach?"

"Of course it didn't happen on the beach. I only meant we walked that way. I left Sarah by the door and went to find the priest. I had to tell him a few lies—white ones of course—to explain things. I could put it all on my husband, of course. I said he'd promised before we married, and then he'd broken his promise. It helped a lot not being able to speak much French. You sound awfully truthful if you don't know the right words. Anyway, he did it there and then, and we caught the bus back to lunch."

"Did what?"

"Baptized her a Catholic."

"Is that all?" I asked with relief.

"Well, it's a sacrament—or so they say."

"I thought at first you meant that Sarah was a real Catholic."

"Well, you see, she was one, only she didn't know it. I wish Henry had buried her properly," Mrs. Bertram said, and began again the grotesque drip of tears.

"You can't blame him if even Sarah didn't know."

"I always had a wish that it would 'take.' Like vaccination."

"It doesn't seem to have taken much with you," I couldn't resist saying, but she wasn't offended. "Oh," she said, "I've had a lot of temptations in my life. I expect things will come right in the end. Sarah was very patient with me. She was a good girl. Nobody appreciated her like I did." She took some more port and said, "If only you'd known her properly. Why, if she'd been brought up in the right way, if I hadn't always married such mean men, she could have been a saint, I truly believe."

"But it just didn't take," I said fiercely and I called the waiter to bring the bill. A wing of those grey geese that fly above our future graves had sent a draught down my back, or else perhaps I had caught a chill in the frozen grounds; if only it could have been a deathly chill like Sarah's.

It didn't take, I repeated to myself all the way home in the tube, after depositing Mrs. Bertram at Marylebone and lending her another three pounds "because tomorrow's Wednesday and I have to stay in for the char." Poor Sarah, what had taken had been that string of husbands and stepfathers. Her mother had taught her effectively enough that one man was not enough for a lifetime, but she herself had seen through the pretence of her mother's marriages. When she married Henry she married for life, as I knew with despair.

But that wisdom had nothing to do with the shifty ceremony near the beach. It wasn't you that took, I told the God I didn't believe in, that imaginary God who Sarah thought had saved my life—for what conceivable purpose?—and who had ruined even in his non-existence the only deep happiness I had ever experienced. Oh, no, it wasn't you that took, for that would have been magic, and I believe in magic even less than I believe in you; magic is your cross, your resurrection of the body, your holy Catholic church, your communion of saints.

I lay on my back and watched the shadows of the Common trees shift on my ceiling. It's just a coincidence, I thought, a horrible coincidence that nearly brought her back at the end to you. You can't mark a two-year-old child for life with a bit of water and a prayer. If I began to believe that, I could believe in the body and the blood. You didn't own her all those years; I owned her. You won in the end, you don't need to remind me of that, but she wasn't deceiving me with you when she lay here with me, on this bed, with this pillow under her back. When she slept, I was with her, not you. It was I who penetrated her, not you.

All the light went out, darkness was over the bed, and

I dreamed I was at a fair with a gun in my hand. I was shooting at bottles that looked as though they were made of glass, but my bullets bounded off them as though they were coated with steel. I fired and fired, and not a bottle could I crack, and at five in the morning I woke with exactly the same thought in my head: for those years you were mine, not his.

V

It had been a macabre joke of mine when I thought that Henry might ask me to share his house. I had not really expected the offer, and when it came I was taken by surprise. Even his visit a week after the funeral was a surprise; he had never been to my house before. I doubt whether he had ever come much nearer to the south side than the night I met him on the Common in the rain. I heard my bell ring and looked out of the window because I didn't want to see visitors—I had an idea it might be Waterbury with Sylvia. The lamp by the plane tree on the pavement picked out Henry's black hat. I went downstairs and opened the door. "I was just passing by," Henry lied.

"Come in."

He stood and dithered awkwardly while I got my drinks out of a cupboard. He said, "You seem interested in General Gordon."

"They want me to do a life."

"Are you going to do it?"

"I suppose so. I don't feel much like work these days."

"It's the same with me," Henry said.

"Is the Royal Commission still sitting?"

"Yes."

"It gives you something to think about."

"Does it? Yes, I suppose it does. Until we stop for lunch."

"It's important work anyway. Here's your sherry."

"It won't make any difference to a single soul."

What a long way Henry had travelled since the complacent photograph in the *Tatler* that had so angered me. I had a picture of Sarah, enlarged from a snapshot, face down on my desk. He turned it over. "I remember taking that," he said. Sarah had told me the photograph had been taken by a woman friend. I suppose she had lied to save my feelings. In the picture she looked younger and happier, but not more lovely, than in the years I had known her. I wished I had been able to make her look that way, but it is the destiny of a lover to watch unhappiness hardening like a cast around his mistress. Henry said, "I was making a fool of myself to make her smile. Is General Gordon an interesting character?"

"In some ways."

Henry said, "The house feels very queer these days. I try to keep out of it as much as possible. I suppose you aren't free for dinner at the club?"

"I've got a lot of work I have to finish."

He looked round my room. He said, "You haven't much space for your books here."

"No. I have to keep some of them under the bed."

He picked up a magazine that Waterbury had sent me before the interview to show an example of his work, and said, "There's room in my house. You could have practically a flat to yourself." I was too astonished to answer. He went rapidly on, turning over the leaves of the magazine as though he were really uninterested in his own suggestion. "Think it over. You mustn't decide now."

"It's very good of you, Henry."

"You'd be doing me a favour, Bendrix."

I thought, why not? Writers are regarded as unconventional. Am I more conventional than a senior civil servant?

"I dreamed last night," Henry said, "about all of us."

"Yes?"

"I don't remember much. We were drinking together. We were happy. When I woke up I thought she wasn't dead."

"I don't dream of her now."

"I wish we'd let that priest have his way."

"It would have been absurd, Henry. She was no more a Catholic than you or me."

"Do you believe in survival, Bendrix?"

"If you mean personal survival, no."

"One can't disprove it, Bendrix."

"It's almost impossible to disprove anything. I write a story. How can you prove that the events in it never happened, that the characters aren't real? Listen. I met a man on the Common today with three legs."

"How terrible," Henry said seriously. "An abortion?"

"And they were covered with fish scales."

"You're joking."

"But prove I am, Henry. You can't disprove my story any more than I can disprove God. But I just know he's a lie, just as you know my story's a lie."

"Of course there are arguments."

"Oh, I could invent a philosophic argument for my story, I daresay, based on Aristotle."

Henry abruptly changed the subject back. "It would save you a bit if you came and stayed with me. Sarah always said your books weren't as successful as they should be."

"Oh, the shadow of success is falling upon them." I thought of Waterbury's article. I said, "A moment comes when you can hear the popular reviewers dipping their pens for the plaudits—even before the next book's written. It's all a question of time." I talked because I hadn't made up my mind.

Henry said, "There's no ill-feeling left, is there, Bendrix? I got angry with you at your club, about that man. But what does it matter now?"

"I was wrong. He was only some crazy tub-thumping rationalist with a strawberry mark all over his cheek. Forget it, Henry."

"She was good, Bendrix. People talk, but she was good. It wasn't her fault that I couldn't—well, love her properly. You know I'm awfully prudent, cautious. I'm not the sort that makes a lover. She wanted somebody like you."

"She left me. She moved on, Henry."

"Do you know, I read one of your books once—Sarah made me. You described a house after a woman in it had died."

"The Ambitious Host."

"That was the name. It seemed all right at the time. I thought it very plausible; but you got it all wrong, Bendrix. You described how the husband found the house terribly empty; he moved about the rooms, shifting chairs, trying to give an effect of another being there. Sometimes he'd pour himself drinks into two glasses."

"I forget it. It sounds a bit literary."

"It's off the mark, Bendrix. The trouble is, the house doesn't seem empty. You see, often in the old days I'd

come home from the office, and she would be out somewhere—perhaps with you. I'd call, and she wouldn't answer. Then the house was empty. I almost expected to
find the furniture gone. You know, I did love her in my
way, Bendrix. Every time she wasn't there when I came
home those last months I dreaded to see a letter waiting
for me. 'Dear Henry'—you know the kind of thing they
write in novels?"

"Yes."

"But now the house never seems empty like that. I
don't know how to express it. Because she's always away,
she's never away. You see, she's never anywhere else.
She's not having lunch with anybody, she's not at a
cinema with you. There's nowhere for her to be but at
home."

"But where's her home?" I said.

"Oh, you've got to forgive me, Bendrix. I'm nervy and
tired; I don't sleep well. You know the next best thing
to talking *to* her is talking about her, and there's only
you."

"She had a lot of friends. Sir William Mallock, Dunstan—"

"I can't talk about her to them. Any more than to that
man Parkis."

"Parkis!" I exclaimed. Had he lodged himself in our
lives forever?

"He told me he'd been at a cocktail party we gave. The
strange people Sarah picked up! He said you knew him
too."

"What on earth did he want with you?"

"He said she'd been kind to his little boy—God knows

when. The boy's sick. He seemed to want something of
hers for a memento. I gave him one or two of her old children's books. There were a lot of them in her room, all
scrawled over in pencil. It was a good way of getting rid
of them. One can't just send them to Foyle's, can one? I
don't see any harm in it, do you?"

"No. That was the man I put to watch her, from Savage's detective agency."

"Good God, if I'd known— But he seemed really fond
of her."

"Parkis is human," I said. "He's easily touched." I
looked around at my room. There wouldn't be any more
of Sarah where Henry came from—less, perhaps, for she
would be diluted there.

"I'll come and stay with you, Henry, but you must let
me pay some rent."

"I'm so glad, Bendrix. But the house is freehold. You
can pay your share of the rates."

"Three months' notice to find new digs when you
marry again."

He took me quite seriously. "I shall never want to do
that. I'm not the marrying kind. It was a great injury
I did to Sarah when I married her. I know that now."

VI

So I moved to the north side of the Common. I wasted
a week's rent because Henry wanted me to come at once,
and I paid five pounds for a van to take my books and
clothes across. I had the guest room, and Henry fitted up
a lumber room as a study, and there was a bath on the
floor above. Henry had moved into his dressing room,
and the room they had shared, with the cold twin beds,
was left for guests who never came. After a few days I
began to see what Henry meant by the house never being
empty. I worked at the British Museum until it closed,
and then I would go back and wait for Henry, and usually we went out and drank a little at the Pontefract
Arms. Once when Henry was away for a few days at
a conference at Bournemouth I picked up a girl and
brought her back. It wasn't any good. I knew it at once.
I was impotent, and to save her feelings I told her that
I had promised a woman I loved never to do this with
anyone else. She was very sweet and understanding about
it; prostitutes have a great respect for sentiment. This
time there had been no revenge in my mind, and I felt
only sadness at abandoning forever something I had enjoyed so much. I dreamed of Sarah afterwards, and we
were lovers again in my old room on the south side,
but again nothing happened, only this time there was no
sadness in the fact. We were happy and without regret.

It was a few days afterwards that I pulled open a cupboard door in my bedroom and found a pile of old children's books. Henry must have looted this cupboard for

Parkis's boy. There were several of Andrew Lang's fairy books in their coloured covers, many Beatrix Potters, *The Children of the New Forest, The Golliwog at the North Pole,* and also one or two older books—Captain Scott's *Last Expedition* and the *Poems* of Thomas Hood, the last bound in school leather with a label saying that it had been awarded to Sarah Bertram for proficiency in algebra. Algebra! How one changes.

I couldn't work that evening. I lay on the floor with the books and tried to trace at least a few features in the blank spaces of Sarah's life. There are times when a lover longs to be also a father and a brother; he is jealous of the years he hasn't shared. *The Golliwog at the North Pole* was probably the earliest of Sarah's books because it had been scrawled all over, this way and that way, meaninglessly, destructively, with coloured chalks. In one of the Beatrix Potters her name had been spelt in pencil, one big capital letter arranged wrongly so that what appeared was SAЯAH. In *The Children of the New Forest* she had written very tidily and minutely, "Sarah Bertram Her Book. Please ask permission to borrow. And if you steal it will be to your sorrow." They were the marks of every child who had ever lived, traces as anonymous as the claw marks of birds that one sees in winter. When I closed the books they were covered at once by the drift of time.

I doubt whether she had ever read Hood's poems; the pages were as clean as when the book was handed to her by the headmistress or the distinguished visitor. Indeed, as I was about to put it back in the cupboard a leaf of print dropped on the floor—the programme, probably, of that very prize-giving. In a handwriting I could recognize—but even our handwriting begins young and takes on the tired arabesques of time—was a phrase: "What utter piffle." I could imagine Sarah writing it down and showing it to her neighbour as the headmistress resumed her seat, applauded respectfully by parents. I don't know why another line of hers came into my head when I saw that schoolgirl phrase with all its impatience, its incomprehension, and its assurance: "I'm a phony and a fake." Here under my hand was innocence. It seemed such a pity that she had lived another twenty years only to feel that about herself. A phony and a fake. Was it a description I had used of her in a moment of anger? She always harboured my criticism; it was only praise that slid from her like the snow.

I turned the leaf over and read the programme of July 23, 1926: the Water Music of Handel played by Miss Duncan, R.C.M.; a recitation of "I wandered lonely as a cloud" by Beatrice Collins; Tudor Ayres by the School Glee Society; Violin Recital of Chopin's Waltz in A Flat by Mary Pippitt. The long summer afternoon of twenty years ago stretched out its shadows towards me, and I hated life that so alters us for the worse. I thought, that summer I had just begun my first novel; there was so much excitement, ambition, hope, when I sat down to work; I wasn't bitter, I was happy. I put the leaf back in the unread book and thrust the volume to the back of the cupboard under the *Golliwog* and the Beatrix Potters. We were both happy with only ten years and a few counties between us, who were later to come together for no apparent purpose but to give each other so much pain. I took up Scott's *Last Expedition*.

That had been one of my own favourite books. It seemed curiously dated now, this heroism with only the ice for enemy, self-sacrifice that involved no deaths beyond one's own. Two wars stood between us and them. I looked at the photographs: the beards and goggles, the little cairns of snow, the Union Jack, the ponies with their long manes like outdated hair dressings among the striped rocks. Even the deaths were "period," and "period" too was the schoolgirl who marked the pages with lines, exclamation marks, who wrote neatly in the margin of Scott's last letter home, "And what comes next? Is it God? Robert Browning." Even then, I thought, *he* came into her mind. He was as underhand as a lover, taking advantage of a passing mood, like a hero seducing us with his improbabilities and his legends. I put the last book back and turned the key in the lock.

VII

"Where have you been, Henry?" I asked. He was usually the first at breakfast and sometimes he had left the house before I came down, but this morning his plate had not been touched, and I heard the front door close softly before he appeared.

"Oh, just down the road," he said vaguely.

"Been out all night?" I asked.

"No. Of course not." To clear himself of that charge he told me the truth. "Father Crompton said Mass today for Sarah."

"Is he still at it?"

"Once a month. I thought it would be polite to look in."

"I don't suppose he'd know you were there."

"I saw him afterwards to thank him. As a matter of fact I asked him to dinner."

"Then I shall go out."

"I wish you wouldn't, Bendrix. After all, in his way, he was a friend of Sarah's."

"You aren't turning a believer too, are you, Henry?"

"Of course I'm not. But they've as much right to their views as we have."

So he came to dinner. Ugly, haggard, graceless with the Torquemada nose, he was the man who had kept Sarah from me. He had supported her in the absurd vow which ought to have been forgotten in a week. It was to his church that she had walked in the rain, seeking a refuge and "catching her death" instead. It was hard for me to show even bare politeness, and Henry had to shoulder the burden of the dinner. Father Crompton was not used to dining out. One had the impression that this was a duty on which he found it hard to keep his mind. He had very limited small talk, and his answers fell like trees across the road.

"You have a good deal of poverty around here, I suppose?" Henry said, rather tired, over the cheese. He had tried so many things—the influence of books, the cinema, a recent visit to France, the possibility of a third war.

"That's not a problem," Father Crompton replied.

Henry worked hard. "Immorality?" he asked with the slightly false note we can't avoid with such a word.

"That's never a problem," Father Crompton said.

"I thought perhaps—the Common—one notices at night—"

"You get it happening with any open space. And it's winter now anyway." And that closed that.

"Some more cheese, Father?"

"No, thank you."

"I suppose in a district like this you have a good deal of trouble raising money—for charity, I mean?"

"People give what they can."

"Some brandy with your coffee?"

"No, thank you."

"You don't mind if we—"

"Of course I don't. I can't get to sleep on it, that's all, and I have to get up at six."

"Whatever for?"

"Prayer. You get used to it."

"I'm afraid I've never been able to pray much," Henry

said, "since I was a boy. I used to pray to get into the second fifteen."

"And did you?"

"I got into the third. I'm afraid that kind of prayer isn't much good, is it, Father?"

"Any kind's better than none. It's a recognition of God's power anyway, and that's a kind of praise, I suppose." I hadn't heard him talk so much since dinner had started.

"I should have thought," I said, "it was more like touching wood or avoiding the lines on the pavement—at that age anyway."

"Oh, well," he said, "I'm not against a bit of superstition. It gives people the idea that this world's not everything." He scowled at me down his nose. "It could be the beginning of wisdom."

"Your church certainly goes in for superstition in a big way—St. Januarius, bleeding statues, visions of the Virgin, that sort of thing."

'We try to sort them out. And isn't it more sensible to believe that *anything* may happen than—"

The bell rang. Henry said, "I told the maid she could go to bed. Would you excuse me, Father?"

"I'll go," I said. I was glad to get away from that oppressive presence. He had the answers too pat; the amateur could never hope to catch him out, he was like a conjuror who bores one by his very skill. I opened the front door and saw a stout woman in black holding a paper parcel. For a moment I thought it was our charwoman until she said, "Are you Mr. Bendrix, sir?"

"Yes."

"I was to give you this." And she thrust the parcel quickly into my hand, as though it contained something explosive.

"Who's it from?"

"Mr. Parkis, sir." I turned it over in perplexity. It even occurred to me that he might have mislaid some evidence which now, too late, he was handing over to me. I wanted to forget Mr. Parkis.

"If you'd give me a receipt, sir? I was to put the parcel into your own hands."

"I haven't a pencil—or paper. I really can't be bothered."

"You know how Mr. Parkis is about records, sir. I've got a pencil in my bag."

I wrote the receipt out for her on the back of a used envelope. She stowed it carefully away and then scuttled to the gate as though she wanted to get as far as possible as quickly as she could. I stood in the hall, weighing the object in my hand. Henry called out to me from the dining room, "What is it, Bendrix?"

"A parcel from Parkis," I said. The phrase sounded like a tongue-twister.

"I suppose he's returning the book."

"At this hour? And it's addressed to me."

"Well, what is it, then?" I didn't want to open the parcel. Weren't we both of us engaged in the painful process of forgetting? I felt as though I had been punished enough for my visit to Mr. Savage's agency. I heard Father Crompton's voice saying, "I ought to be off now, Mr. Miles."

"It's early yet."

I thought, if I stay out of the room, I shan't have to add my politeness to Henry's, he may go sooner. I opened the parcel.

Henry was right. It was one of the Andrew Lang fairy books, but a piece of folded notepaper stuck out between the leaves. It was a letter from Parkis.

"Dear Mr. Bendrix," I read, and, thinking it was a note of thanks, my eyes impatiently took in the last sentences. "So under the circumstances I would rather not have the book in the house and hoping that you will explain to Mr. Miles that there is no ingratitude on the part of yours truly, Alfred Parkis."

I sat down in the hall. I heard Henry say, "Don't think I've got a closed mind, Father Crompton"—and I began to read Parkis's letter from the beginning.

"Dear Mr. Bendrix, I am writing to you and not Mr. Miles being assured of your sympathy due to our close even though sad association and you being a literary gentleman of imagination and accustomed to strange events. You know my boy has been bad lately with awful pains in his stomach and not being due to ice cream I have been afraid of appendicitis. The doctor said operate, it can't do any harm, but I have great fear of the knife for my poor boy, his mother having died under it due to negligence I am sure, and what would I do if I lost my boy the same way? I would be quite alone. Forgive all the details, Mr. Bendrix, but in my profession we are trained to put things in order and explain first things first, so the judge can't complain he hasn't been given the facts plainly. So I said to the doctor on Monday, let's wait until we are quite certain. Only I think sometimes it was the cold that did it and he waiting and watching outside Mrs. Miles's house, and you will forgive me if I say she was a lady of great kindness who deserved to be left alone. You can't pick and choose in my job, but ever since that first day in Maiden Lane I wished it was any other lady I had the watching of. Anyway my boy was upset terribly when he heard how the poor lady had died. She only spoke to him once, but somehow he got the idea, I think, that his mother had been like her, only she wasn't, though a good true woman in her way too whom I miss every day of my life. Well, when his temperature was 103 which is high for a boy like him, he began to talk to Mrs. Miles just the same as he had done in the street, but he told her he was watching her which of course he wouldn't do, having professional pride even at his age. Then he began to cry when she went away, and then he slept, but when he woke up, his temperature being still 102, he asked for the present she had promised him in the dream. So that was why I bothered Mr. Miles and deceived him of which I am ashamed there not being a professional reason, only my poor boy.

"When I got the book and gave it him he became calmer. But I was worried because the doctor said he would not take any more risks and he must go to hospital on Wednesday and if there had been an empty bed he would have sent him that night. So you see I couldn't sleep for worrying because of my poor wife and my poor boy and being afraid of the knife. I don't mind telling *you,* Mr. Bendrix, that I prayed very hard. I prayed to God and then I prayed to my wife to do what she could because if there's anyone in Heaven, she's in Heaven now, and I asked Mrs. Miles, if she was there, to do what she could too. Now if a grown man can do that, Mr. Bendrix, you can understand my poor boy imagining things. When I woke up this morning, his temperature was 99 and he hadn't any pain, and when the doctor came there wasn't any tenderness left, so he says we can wait awhile and he's been all right all day. Only he told the doctor it was Mrs. Miles who came and took away the pain—touching him on the right side of the stomach if you'll forgive the indelicacy—and she wrote in the book for him. But the doctor says he must be kept very quiet and the book excites him, so under the circumstances I would rather not have the book in the house . . ."

When I turned the letter over there was a postscript: "There is something written in the book, but anyone can see that was many years ago when Mrs. Miles was a little girl, only I can't explain that to my poor boy for fear the pain might return. Respectfully, A.P." I turned to the flyleaf, and there was the unformed scribble with indelible pencil, just as I had seen it before in the other books in which the child Sarah Bertram had composed her mottoes.

When I was ill my mother gave me this book by Lang,
If any well person steals it he will get a great bang,
But if you are sick in bed
You can have it to read instead.

I carried it back with me into the dining room.

"What was it?" Henry asked.

"The book," I said. "Did you read what Sarah had written in it before you gave it to Parkis?"

"No. Why?"

"A coincidence, that's all. But it seems you don't need to belong to Father Crompton's persuasion to be superstitious." I gave Henry the letter. He read it and handed it to Father Crompton.

"I don't like it," Henry said. "Sarah's dead. I hate to see her being bandied about."

"I know what you mean. I feel it too."

"It's like hearing her discussed by strangers."

"They aren't saying anything ill of her," Father Crompton said. He laid the letter down. "I must go now." But he made no move, looking at the letter on the table. He asked, "And the inscription?"

I pushed the book across to him. "Oh, it was written years ago. She wrote that kind of thing in a lot of her books, like all children."

"Time's a strange thing," Father Crompton said.

"Of course the child wouldn't understand it was all done in the past."

"St. Augustine asked where time came from. He said it came out of the future which didn't exist yet, into the present that had no duration, and went into the past which had ceased to exist. I don't know that we can understand time any better than a child."

"I didn't mean—"

"Oh, well," Father Crompton said, standing up, "you mustn't take this to heart, Mr. Miles. It only goes to show what a good woman your wife was."

"That's no help to me, is it? She's part of the past that has ceased to exist."

"The man who wrote that letter had a lot of sense in

him. There's no harm in praying to the dead as well as for them." He repeated his phrase. "She was a good woman."

Quite suddenly I lost my temper. I believe I was annoyed chiefly by his complacency, the sense that nothing intellectual could ever trouble him, the assumption of an intimate knowledge of somebody he had known only for a few hours or days, whom we had known for years. I said, "She was nothing of the sort."

"Bendrix!" Henry said sharply.

"She could put blinkers on any man," I said, "even on a priest. She's only deceived you, Father, as she deceived her husband and me. She was a consummate liar."

"She never pretended to be what she wasn't."

"I wasn't her only lover—"

"Stop it!" Henry said. "You've no right—"

"Let him alone," Father Crompton said. "Let the poor man rave."

"Don't give me your professional pity, Father. Keep it for your penitents."

"You can't dictate to me whom I'm to pity, Mr. Bendrix."

"Any man could have her." I longed to believe what I said, for then there would be nothing to miss or regret. I would no longer be tied to her, wherever she was. I would be free.

"And you can't teach me anything about penitence, Mr. Bendrix. I've had twenty-five years of the Confessional. There's nothing we can do some of the saints haven't done before us."

"I've got nothing to repent except failure. Go back to

your own people, Father, back to your bloody little box
and your beads."

"You'll find me there any time you want me."

"Me want you, Father? Father, I don't want to be rude,
but I'm no Sarah. No Sarah."

Henry said with embarrassment, "I'm sorry, Father."

"You don't need to be. I know when a man's in pain."

I couldn't get through the tough skin of his complacency. I pushed my chair back and said, "You're wrong,
Father. This isn't anything subtle like pain. I'm not in
pain, I'm in hate. I hate Sarah because she was a whore,
I hate Henry because she stuck to him, and I hate you
and your imaginary God because you took her away from
all of us."

"You're a good hater," Father Crompton said.

Tears stood in my eyes because I was powerless to hurt
any of them. "To hell with the lot of you," I said.

I slammed the door behind me and shut them in together. Let him spill his holy wisdom to Henry, I
thought. I'm alone. I want to be alone. If I can't have you,
I'll be alone always. Oh, I'm as capable of belief as the
next man. I would only have to shut the eyes of my mind
for a long enough time, and I could believe that you came
to Parkis's boy in the night with your touch that brings
peace. Last month in the crematorium I asked you to
save that girl from me, and you pushed your mother between us—or so they might say. But if I start believing
that, then I have to believe in your God. I'd have to love
your God. I'd rather love the men you slept with.

I've got to be reasonable, I told myself, going upstairs.
Sarah has been dead a long time now; one doesn't go on

loving the dead with this intensity, only the living, and she's not alive, she can't be alive. I mustn't believe that she's alive. I lay down on my bed and closed my eyes and I tried to be reasonable. If I hate her so much as I sometimes do, how can I love her? Can one really hate and love? Or is it only myself that I really hate? I hate the books I write with their trivial unimportant skill; I hate the craftsman's mind in me, so greedy for copy that I set out to seduce a woman I didn't love for the information she could give me; I hate this body that enjoyed so much but was inadequate to express what the heart felt; and I hate my untrusting mind that set Parkis on the watch, who laid powder on doorbells, rifled waste-paper baskets, stole your secrets.

From the drawer of my bedside table I took her journal and, opening it at random, under a date last October, I read, "O God, if I could really hate you, what would that mean?" And I thought, hating Sarah is only loving Sarah, and hating myself is only loving myself. I'm not worth hating—Maurice Bendrix, author of *The Ambitious Host, The Crowned Image, The Grave on the Waterfront*—Bendrix the scribbler. Nothing, not even Sarah, is worth our hatred if You exist, except You. "I thought, sometimes I've hated Maurice, but would I have hated him if I hadn't loved him too? O God, if I could really hate you . . ."

I remembered how Sarah had prayed to the God she didn't believe in, and now I spoke to the Sarah I didn't believe in. I said, You sacrificed both of us once to bring me back to life, but what sort of a life is this without you? It's all very well for you to love God. You are dead. You have Him. But I'm sick with life, I'm rotten with health. If I begin to love God, I can't just die. I've got to do something about it. I had to touch you with my hands, I had to taste you with my tongue; one can't love and do nothing. It's no use your telling me not to worry as you did once in a dream. If I ever loved like that, it would be the end of everything. Loving you, I had no appetite for food, I felt no lust for any other woman, but loving Him there'd be no pleasure in anything at all with Him away. I'd even lose my work, I'd cease to be Bendrix. Sarah, I'm afraid.

That night I came wide awake at two in the morning. I went down to the larder and got myself some biscuits and a drink of water. I was sorry I had spoken like that about Sarah in front of Henry. The priest had said there was nothing we could do that some saint had not done. That might be true of murder and adultery, the spectacular sins, but could a saint ever have been guilty of envy and meanness? My hate was as petty as my love. I opened the door softly and looked in at Henry. He lay asleep, with the light on and his arm shielding his eyes. With the eyes hidden there was an anonymity about the whole body. He was just a man—one of us. He was like the first enemy soldier a man encounters on a battlefield, dead and indistinguishable, not a White or a Red, but just a human being like himself. I put two biscuits by his bed, in case he woke, and turned the light out.

VIII

My book wasn't going well (what a waste of time the act of writing seemed, but I knew no other way of using time) and I took a walk across the Common to listen to the speakers. There was a man I remembered who used to amuse me in the prewar days, and I was glad to see him safely back on his pitch. He had no message to convey like the political and the religious speakers. He was an ex-actor and he just told stories and recited snatches of verse. He would challenge his audience to catch him out by asking for any piece of verse. "The Ancient Mariner," somebody would call, and at once, with great emphasis, he would give us a quatrain. One wag said, "Shakespeare's Thirty-second Sonnet," and he recited four lines at random, and when the wag objected he said, "You've got the wrong edition." I looked around at my fellow listeners and saw Smythe. Perhaps he had seen me first, for he had the handsome side of his face turned towards me, the side Sarah had not kissed, but if so he avoided my eye.

Why did I always wish to speak to anybody whom Sarah had known? I pushed my way to his side and said, "Hullo, Smythe." He clamped a handkerchief to the bad side of his face and turned towards me. "Oh, it's Mr. Bendrix," he said.

"I haven't seen you since the funeral."

"I've been away."

"Don't you still speak here?"

"No." He hesitated and then added unwillingly, "I've given up public speaking."

"But you still give home tuition?" I teased him.

"No. I've given that up too."

"Not changed your views, I hope?"

He said gloomily, "I don't know what to believe."

"Nothing. Surely that was the point."

"It was." He began to move a little way out of the crowd, and I found myself on his bad side. I couldn't resist teasing him a little more. "Have you got toothache?" I asked.

"No. Why?"

"It looked like it. With that handkerchief."

He didn't reply but took the handkerchief away. There was no ugliness to hide. His skin was fresh and young except for a small blue patch no larger than a half-crown.

He said, "I get tired of explaining when I meet people I know."

"You found a cure?"

"Yes. I told you I've been away."

"To a nursing home?"

"Yes."

"Operation?"

"Not exactly." He added unwillingly, "It was done by touch."

"Faith healing?"

"I have no faith. I'd never go to a quack."

"I never knew a cure was possible."

He said vaguely, to close the subject, "Modern methods. Electricity."

I went back home and again I tried to settle to my book. Always I find when I begin to write there is one character who obstinately will not come alive. There is nothing psychologically false about him, but he sticks, he has to be pushed around, words have to be found for him, all the technical skill I have acquired through the laborious years has to be employed in making him appear alive to my readers. Sometimes I get a sour satisfaction when a reviewer praises him as the best-drawn character in the story; if he has not been drawn he has certainly been dragged. He lies heavily on my mind whenever I start to work, like an ill-digested meal on the stomach, robbing me of the pleasure of creation in any scene where he is present. He never does the unexpected thing, he never surprises me, he never takes charge. Every other character helps, he only hinders.

And yet one cannot do without him. I can imagine a God feeling in just that way about some of us. The saints, one would suppose, in a sense create themselves. They come alive. They are capable of the surprising act or word. They stand outside the plot, unconditioned by it. But we have to be pushed around. We have the obstinacy of non-existence. We are inextricably bound to the plot, and wearily God forces us, here and there, according to his intention, characters without poetry, without free will, whose only importance is that somewhere, at some time, we help to furnish the scene in which a living character moves and speaks, providing perhaps the saints with the opportunities for their free will.

I was glad when I heard the door close and Henry's footsteps in the hall. It was an excuse to stop. That character could remain inert now till morning; it was the hour at last for the Pontefract Arms. I waited for him to call up to me—already in a month we were as set in our ways as two bachelors who have lived together for years—but he didn't call, and I heard him go into his study. After a while I followed him—I missed my drink.

I was reminded of the occasion when I had come back with him first; he sat there beside the green Discus Thrower, worried and dejected, but now, watching him, I felt neither envy nor pleasure.

"A drink, Henry?"

"Yes, yes. Of course. I was only going to change my shoes." He had his town and his country shoes, and the Common, in his eyes, was country. He bent over his laces; there was a knot that he couldn't untie—he was always bad with his fingers. He got tired of struggling and wrenched the shoe off. I picked it up and uncoiled the knot for him.

"Thank you, Bendrix." Perhaps even so small an act of companionship gave him confidence. "A very unpleasant thing happened today at the office," he said.

"Tell me."

"Mrs. Bertram called. I don't think you know Mrs. Bertram."

"Oh, yes. I met her the other day." A curious phrase, the other day, as though all days were the same except that one.

"We've never got on very well together."

"So she told me."

"Sarah was always very good about it. She kept her away."

"Did she come to borrow money?"

"Yes. She wanted ten pounds—her usual story: in town for the day, shopping, run out, banks closed. Bendrix, I'm not a mean man, but I get so irritated by the way she goes on. She has two thousand a year of her own. It's almost as much as I earn."

"Did you give it her?"

"Oh, yes. One always does, but the trouble was I couldn't resist a sermon. That made her furious. I told her how many times she'd done it and how many times she had paid me back—that was easy: the first time. She took out her cheque book and said she was going to write me a cheque for the whole lot there and then. She was so angry that I'm certain she meant it. She'd really forgotten that she had used her last cheque. She had meant to humiliate me and she only succeeded in humiliating herself, poor woman. Of course that made it worse."

"What did she do?"

"She accused me of not giving Sarah a proper funeral. She told me a strange story."

"I know it. She told it to me after a couple of ports."

"Do you think she's lying?"

"No."

"It's an extraordinary coincidence, isn't it? Baptized at two years old, and then beginning to go back to what you can't even remember— It's like an infection."

"It's what you say, an odd coincidence." Once before I had supplied Henry with the necessary strength; I wasn't going to let him weaken now. "I've known stranger coincidences," I went on. "During the last year, Henry, I've been so bored I've even collected car numbers. That teaches you about coincidences. Ten thousand possible numbers and God knows how many combinations, and yet over and over again I've seen two cars with the same figures side by side in a traffic block."

"Yes. I suppose it works that way."

"I'll never lose my faith in coincidence, Henry."

The telephone was ringing faintly upstairs; we hadn't heard it till now because the switch was turned off in the study.

"Oh, dear, oh, dear," Henry said. "I wouldn't be a bit surprised if it were that woman again."

"Let her ring." And as I spoke the bell stopped.

"It isn't that I'm mean," Henry said. "I don't suppose she's borrowed more than a hundred pounds in ten years."

"Come out and have a drink."

"Of course. Oh, I haven't put on my shoes." He bent over them, and I could see the bald patch on the crown of his head; it was as though his worries had worn through —I had been one of his worries. He said, "I don't know what I'd do without you, Bendrix."

I brushed a few grains of scurf off his shoulder. "Oh, well, Henry—" And then, before we could move, the bell began to ring again.

"Leave it," I said.

"I'd better answer. You don't know—" He got up, his shoelaces dangling, and came over to his desk. "Hullo," he said, "Miles speaking." He passed the receiver to me and said with relief, "It's for you."

"Yes," I said, "Bendrix here."

"Mr. Bendrix," a man's voice said, "I felt I'd got to ring you. I didn't tell you the truth this afternoon."

"Who *are* you?"

"Smythe," the voice said.

"I don't understand."

"I told you I'd been to a nursing home. I never went to one."

"Really, it couldn't matter less to me."

His voice reached for me along the line. "Of course it matters. You aren't listening to me. Nobody treated my face. It cleared up suddenly, in a night."

"How? I still don't—"

He said with an awful air of conspiracy, "You and I know how. There's no getting round it. It wasn't right of me, keeping it dark. It was a—" but I put down the receiver before he could use that foolish newspaper word that was the alternative to "coincidence." I remembered his clenched right hand, I remembered my anger that the dead can be so parcelled up, divided like their clothes. I thought, he's so proud that he must always have some kind of revelation. In a week or two he'll be speaking about it on the Common and showing his healed face. It will be in the newspapers "Rationalist Speaker Converted by Miraculous Cure." I tried to summon up all my faith in coincidence, but all I could think of, and that with envy, for I had no relic, was the ruined cheek lying at night on her hair.

"Who is it?" Henry asked. I hesitated a moment whether to tell him, but then I thought, no. I don't trust him. He and Father Crompton will get together.

"Smythe," I said.

"Smythe?"

"That fellow Sarah used to visit."

"What did he want?"

"His face has been cured, that's all. I asked him to let me know the name of the specialist. I have a friend—"

"Do you mean they've grafted skin?"

"I'm not sure. I've read somewhere these marks are hysterical in origin. A mixture of psychiatry and radium." It sounded plausible. Perhaps after all it was the truth—another coincidence; two cars with the same number plate. And with a sense of weariness I thought, how many coincidences are there going to be? Her mother at the funeral, the child's dream. Is this going to continue day by day? I felt like a swimmer who has overpassed his strength and knows the tide is stronger than himself, but if I drowned I was going to hold Henry up till the last moment. Wasn't it after all the duty of a friend, for if this thing were not disproved, if it got into the papers, nobody could tell where it would end? I remembered the roses at Manchester; that fraud had taken a long time to be recognized for what it was. People are so hysterical in these days. There might be relic-hunters, prayers, processions. Henry was not unknown; the scandal would be enormous. And all the journalists, asking questions about their life together and digging out that queer story of the baptism near Deauville—the vulgarity of the pious press. I could imagine the headlines, and the headlines would produce more "miracles." We had to kill this thing at the start.

I remembered the journal in my drawer upstairs and I thought, that has to go too, for that could be interpreted in their way. It was as though to save her for ourselves we had to destroy her features one by one. Even her children's books had proved a danger. There were photographs—the one Henry had taken; the press mustn't have that. Was Maud to be trusted? The two of us had tried to build a makeshift house together, and even that was being broken up.

"What about our drink?" Henry said.

"I'll join you in a minute."

I went up to my room and took the journal out. I tore the covers off. They were tough; the cotton backing came out like fibres; it was like tearing the limbs off a bird, and there the journal lay on the bed, a pad of paper, wingless and wounded. The last page lay upwards, and I read again: "You were there, teaching us to squander, . . . so that one day we might have nothing left except this love of You. But You are too good to me. When I ask You for pain, You give me peace. Give it him too. Give him my peace—he needs it more."

You've failed there, Sarah, I thought. One of your prayers at least has not been answered. I have no peace and I have no love, except for you, you. I said to her, I'm a man of hate. But I didn't feel much hatred; I had called other people hysterical, but my own words were overcharged. I could detect their insincerity. What I chiefly felt was less hate than fear. For if this God exists, I thought, and if even you—with your lusts and your adulteries and the timid lies you used to tell—can change like this, we could all be saints by leaping as you leapt, by shutting the eyes and leaping once and for all; if *you* are a saint, it's not so difficult to be a saint. It's something He can demand of any of us—leap! But I won't leap.

I sat on my bed and said to God, You've taken her but

You haven't got me yet. I know Your cunning. It's You who take us up to a high place and offer us the whole universe. You're a devil, God, tempting us to leap. But I don't want Your peace and I don't want Your love. I wanted something very simple and very easy: I wanted Sarah for a lifetime, and You took her away. With Your great schemes You ruin our happiness as a harvester ruins a mouse's nest. I hate You, God, I hate You as though You existed.

I looked at the pad of paper. It was more impersonal than a scrap of hair. You can touch hair with your lips and fingers, and I was tired to death of the mind. I had lived for her body and I wanted her body. But the journal was all I had, so I shut it back in the cupboard, for wouldn't that have been one more victory for Him, to destroy it and leave myself more completely without her? All right, have it *your* way, I said to Sarah. I believe you live and that He exists, but it will take more than your prayers to turn this hatred of Him into love. He robbed me, and like that king you wrote about I'll rob Him of what He wants in me. I can't be cured like Smythe and Parkis's boy. Hatred is in my brain, not in my stomach or my skin. It can't be removed like a strawberry mark or an ache. Didn't I hate you as well as love you? And don't I hate myself?

I called down to Henry, "I'm ready," and we walked side by side over the Common towards the Pontefract Arms. The lights were out, and lovers met where the roads intersected, and on the other side of the grass was the house with the ruined steps where He gave me back this hopeless crippled life.

"I look forward to these evening walks of ours," Henry said.

"Yes."

I thought, in the morning I'll ring up a doctor and ask him whether any treatment exists. And then I thought, better not. As long as one doesn't know one can imagine innumerable cures. I put my hand on Henry's arm and held it there; I had to be strong for both of us now, and he wasn't seriously worried yet.

"They are the only things I do look forward to," Henry said.

I wrote at the start that this was a record of hate, and, walking there beside Henry towards the evening glass of beer, I found the one prayer that seemed to serve the winter mood: O God, You've done enough, You've robbed me of enough. I'm too tired and old to learn to love. Leave me alone forever.

function of miracles: to help convert Bendrix

fideism - belief just for the sake of belief
mere will y power to believe is enough, don't
need any justification.

2 views of miracles
1) accept miraculous cuz one believes
2) believes because of the miraculous.

all result of vow she made when thought Maurice dead

Sarah dies "he who loses his life shall find d
save it" — she saves her life by losing it

Victory over death - prob. in Christian lit.
entry way into some other realm

Theme of death y life runs thru Sarah's spiritual
existence
Sarah's journal - death of old Sarah, rebirth of a
new Sarah - not simple easy matter
genuine rebirth

Bendrix - begins w/notion of hate, then feels has to protec
him; reconciled thru Sarah's death
sacrifical death that reconciles people
analog to death of Christ on cross

god that greene has controlling peo allows anyone
to perform miracles
journal - leads to understanding of her

Bendrix wants her cremated to get rid of cher
even tho' cremated, not gotten rid of

Sarah driven to accept arguments by despair

theological - motive for novel